CW00405871

The
with a voice

PEGGY WOODFORD

Oxfordshire WITHDRAWN FOR SALE Co: Libraries
1 9 JUL 1998
J 50p

THE BODLEY HEAD
LONDON   SYDNEY
TORONTO

Acknowledgements are due to the
following for kind permission to reproduce
copyright material:
Belwin-Mills Music Limited, 250 Purley
Way, Croydon, Surrey, England, for the
lyrics of *Donna Donna* © 1940, 1956
Mills Music Inc., New York, All rights
reserved; Tom Paxton and Harmony Music
Ltd for the lyrics of *Going to the Zoo*;
Warner Brothers Music Limited for *Don't
think twice it's all right* by Bob Dylan.

OXFORDSHIRE
COUNTY
LIBRARIES

1 845045 08

British Library Cataloguing
in Publication Data
Woodford, Peggy
The girl with a voice – (New adults)
I. Title   II. Series
823'.914 [F]   PR6073.0615/
ISBN 0-370-30423-3

© Peggy Woodford 1981
Printed in Great Britain for
The Bodley Head Ltd
9 Bow Street, London WC2E 7AL
by Spottiswoode Ballantyne Ltd.,
Colchester and London
Phototypeset in Linotron 202 Sabon by
Western Printing Services Ltd, Bristol
First published 1981

For Alison, Frances and Imogen

1

'Red hair really turns me on.' Claudia stood behind Rod as he sat by the huge deal table. She lowered a colander onto his head like a crown. 'You must admit, Nora, Rod's got beautiful hair.'

'Stop pestering the poor fellow; he isn't used to your mad ways yet.' Nora heaved a saucepan containing boiled potatoes for fifty people over to the sink. 'And I need that colander.'

Rod watched clouds of steam swirl round the two women as they manoeuvred the heavy pan; the kitchen window behind them misted over, hiding the view of the moors. Since his arrival at King's Thornton at teatime Rod had remained in the kitchen, listening to Claudia's vivid chatter. He had never met a girl like her before; he found it difficult to take his eyes off her.

'As you're in such high fettle, mash the spuds. That should use up some of your energy.' Nora turned to open the capacious oven, releasing appetizing smells. 'The meat pies will be ready in five minutes.'

Claudia poured a pint of milk with a flourish onto the hot potatoes.

'*Pow!*' She plunged the masher down. Liquid squirted all over the table, some of it landing on Rod. He laughed as he licked his hand.

'Jeepers. I am sorry.'

'I don't mind.'

'You may not mind, but I do.' Nora was cross. 'Stop showing off, Claudia, and get on with your work.'

Claudia began to mash the potatoes efficiently, smiling to herself. Her shirt sleeves were rolled above her elbows; her arms were very white, with a light sprinkling of freckles. Rod talked to Nora, but his glance was fixed on those slim, strong arms. Claudia enchanted him. When she left the house at eight o'clock, her day's work done, he felt bereft. His own job did not start until next day. He wandered disconsolately about, not knowing the evening's routines, and too shy to ask. The boys were everywhere, playing table tennis, watching television, arguing, doing nothing. At nine-thirty a bell clanged and they were sent to bed, thundering up the uncarpeted wooden stairs.

As the noise died down, Rod stood in the hall gazing at a large, clumsy painting of the house as it had been fifty years before. King's Thornton, home for two hundred years of the Thornton family, had looked very different then. The house was now owned by the local education authority; lawns had become games pitches; asphalt covered the old rose beds. But at least behind the house the moors were as they always had been, brown above the highest horizontal line of drystone walls, mixtures of green—acid, bottle, emerald, and khaki—below.

'Join us for a cup of tea?'

Rod jumped; Dick Lawrence's plimsolls had silenced his approach. 'Thanks.'

'The staff usually congregate in the kitchen after the little bleeders have gone to bed. Follow me.' Dick was a community worker from Sheffield.

In the kitchen were Nora Dilks, the matron-cum-cook, and Kevin Marshall, who like Rod was a volunteer, receiving board, lodging and pocket money for helping with the summer season of 'adventure' holidays for boys from deprived homes. Kevin had ignored Rod since his arrival; Rod disliked him as instinctively as he had liked Claudia.

'Sugar? Biscuit?'

'Thanks.'

'Nora makes the biscuits.' Dick ate two at a time.

'I shan't bother if you wolf them like that.'

'Where do you come from then, Bob?'

'Rod. From London.'

'First visit up north, is it?' Nora swung a mug of tea his way; her hands were small and red. A bent cigarette hung from her lips.

'Yes. I've always wanted to visit Yorkshire.'

'The Dales are great.' Dick belched. 'You've come to the best part. I never get tired of this area, never. It sort of gets you.'

Kevin stared at Dick's cheerful face with an air of silent disagreement.

'Kevin's a Yorkshire lad too, comes from Richmond. Mad about Yorkshire, our Kevin is.' Nora laughed her hacking smoker's laugh.

'Sodding place.' Kevin put his mug in the sink and left the kitchen. Those were the only words Rod had heard him say. Nora went on laughing.

'I sometimes wonder how we stand Kevin,' said Dick.

'He's all right. He just doesn't like wasting words. He's good at his job, say what you like. The boys will follow him any-where. My Jimmy worships the earth he treads.' Nora had a ten-year-old illegitimate son who was the main reason for her taking this holiday job.

'Kevin's a trainee physical education instructor, Rod. He's one of those guys who can run up a mountain and look as if they just got up out of a chair. I reckon the boys worship his muscles.'

'Maybe they do. But he's the only one here who can keep order—he's just got to say jump and they jump.' Nora washed the mugs and hung her apron up. 'I'm off to bed. Have to get up at six.'

Dick and Rod were left, nervously trying to be relaxed together.

'Where does Claudia fit in?'

'She mainly helps Nora in the kitchen. She lives down in the village.' He hesitated, kicking the table leg with his foot. 'I think she just needs the extra money. She's got a wicked tongue in her head, but everyone likes her.' Dick smiled, then yawned. 'You never know what she's going to say or do next. But she's a hard worker, whatever mood she's in.' Dick had a flat classless voice and an unfailingly cheerful manner. His whole being suggested good humour backed by ineptitude. Rod had seen him under a heap of teasing boys that afternoon; he emerged laughing, but the joke had clearly gone too far.

Rod wanted to ask more questions about Claudia, but Dick was back on Kevin. 'He's an arrogant bugger. You can see he thinks he's a cut above everyone. And he *never* talks, never— I've only heard him say about three words at a time, and there are days when he doesn't speak to the staff at all. It makes me uneasy, it really does. I'm a compulsive talker myself, I know; there's nothing I like better than a good discussion on an interesting topic—education, politics, science fiction—I could talk all night. But Kevin doesn't find any topic interesting. Nothing makes him talk.'

'Perhaps he's interested, but just likes listening.'

'If he's interested he makes a good job of hiding it. I don't dislike him, mind. He just unnerves me. Makes me say stupid things.'

'I know the feeling. Does Claudia—?'

'I'm glad you've joined us. It'll be nice to have an ally, someone I can really talk to.'

When Rod finally got himself to bed, he sat on the hard, lumpy mattress in his tiny attic room and didn't feel like an ally. He was afraid Dick's ebullience was going to be as wearing as Kevin's silence. He took out his guitar and played it quietly. He had been asked to lead a folk-song session the following day; the boys had shouted one or two suggestions and he went through the chords of *Foggy, Foggy Dew* and *Frankie and Johnny* before choosing some more songs he thought they might like.

There was a tap on the door. Kevin stood outside. Rod expected him to complain, but instead he asked:

'Know any Beatles songs? *Day Tripper*?'

10

'Not well. I'll have a go. Come in a minute.' Rod hummed and played a few exploratory chords.

'Yeah. That's it.' Kevin went to the dormer window and stood staring out into the darkness while Rod played and sang what he could remember of *Day Tripper*. At the end Kevin said nothing. Rod started on another Beatles song to fill the silence; Kevin turned and with a brief gesture of thanks left the room. Rod heard a door close further down the corridor.

His concentration gone, he put his guitar away in its case and stood as Kevin had, gazing out of the window. He could hear boys whispering and laughing in a room below his. Out across the valley, the moors were dark against the moonlit sky; two miles away, at the mouth of the valley, the lights of Thornton village winked through the swaying trees. Claudia lived down there.

The noise from the dining room was deafening: it was as if a thousand boys, not forty, were shouting as they ate. Dick tried in vain to keep order. Rain beat against the windows; loose casements all over the house rattled in the wind.

Rod took his bacon and eggs from Nora at the hatch.

'Sleep well, Rod?'

'Yes, thanks.'

'They're always noisy when the weather's bad. And it's like November outside, not August. Makes you despair. Jimmy, fetch some more bread, please.'

Her son passed behind her; there was no sign of Claudia in the kitchen. Rod went and sat down under the grey window and began to eat. Dick came and sat beside him; the noise boiled round them.

'Would you mind doing your song session this morning? Kevin's switched his outing to the afternoon, in case it clears up.'

'O.K.' Rod felt a strong attack of nerves; he had never had to deal with a large group of children before.

'After the coffee break then. They'll be doing work on their projects first.' Dick stood up and clapped his hands. 'Shut up, everybody. How can I tell you today's plans if you make such a racket?' A piece of bread hit his ear. 'No missiles, if you don't mind.'

Rod's guitar session went well, particularly after the boys discovered that he had played in his school rock group.

'Do us a number then. Go on.' Voices urged from all over the room.

'Only if you promise not to make any din. If you all shout and yell, I stop. I mean it.'

The boys fell silent. In eager expectation they gazed at Rod; grubby, untidy, unwashed, they were his fans. He swallowed. As the least experienced and proficient member of an in-different group, adulation had not come his way before. He plunged into the most energetic of his repertoire.

The door opened; for a moment he thought it was Claudia and almost faltered. But it was Nora, laughing raucously.

'I see. I see. Rod the Rocker is with us.' She came in clapping her hands and gyrating her hips. Everybody started to sing, and the uproar only ended with the sound of a bell being rung in the hall. Nora hurried back to the kitchen; Rod hoped his activities would be reported back to Claudia, and looked eagerly for her when he collected his food. There was no sign of her. He was convinced she had left for ever.

'Where's Claudia?'

'Day off. Never comes Wednesdays.' Nora slapped potato onto his plate. 'Gives me a chance to recover from the ordeal of her company. Next . . .'

Rod sat down beside Kevin, smiling in his relief. Kevin did not smile back, but stopped his tidy eating long enough to pass the salt and ketchup along the table. He was already dressed in his lightweight orange anorak, walking boots and heavy socks. After lunch he removed the boys for their wet afternoon's trek; dressed in a motley of rainwear and muddy wellingtons, they trailed after him up onto the moor. A beautiful silence filled the house.

12

*

Rod walked down the dale to the village, Claudia's village, in search of toothpaste and stamps. Thornton was small; its one main street contained a general store-cum-post office, a butcher (closed), a bank (open only on Tuesdays), and the Thornton pub with a racehorse and jockey painted on its sign. The grey stone houses of Thornton looked secretive; behind them, well hidden, was a church; Rod could just see the spire. He wandered aimlessly, hoping that Claudia's vivid face would suddenly appear and . . . But even if she did appear, what good would it do him? She would smile and hurry on. He sat in the centre of the market place and ate a bar of chocolate; a party of holiday-makers dressed for the rain ambled past him. He felt isolated, depressed, even threatened by his new surroundings. Quickly, he got up and decided he would look at the church. A guidebook he had glanced at in the post office said it was of great interest.

He squeezed through the gap between two curved old stones at the side of the churchyard gate; these prevented the sheep that grazed the churchyard from escaping but just allowed the passage of a human leg. Gusts of rain sent him hurrying into the empty church. Yet it was the fullest, most cluttered church he had ever seen: built early in the fifteenth century, it had been left undisturbed at the Reformation, and at no time had been rebuilt or structurally modernized. Rod stood bombarded by the haphazard and historical richness; by the strange family pews like theatre boxes, by a solid poor-box with its massive ironwork, by the helms and armour and tattered banners above him, by the faint painting of the Fall on one wall, by the earnest reminders in brass, marble or glass of the Thornton family's piety in life; by the early clarinet used, as its case informed him, to accompany services before the organ was built in 1860.

While Rod was examining the clarinet, a wild-headed man hurried into the church, disappeared for a moment, reappeared holding an electric kettle, and said as he departed: 'Good

13

afternoon. Don't miss the misericords.' Rod had been about to leave; now he hesitated. Increased gusts of rain beat on the windows. He turned and went to the choirstalls, raised the seats, and found the misericords. They were indeed remarkable: he knelt and examined a pelican feeding her young, a mermaid holding a mirror and hairbrush, two pigs dancing to a bagpipe; a fox preaching to chickens and geese; and finally a man in monk's habit sitting in a low doorway, writing. The man's expression was extraordinary: a combination of toughness, sanctity, humour and love. Rod stared at the man's face for some time; whoever had carved it over four hundred years ago had been a master. A booklet at the back told him the monk so magically presented was Richard Rolle, the Yorkshire mystic, who died of the plague in 1349. The misericords were believed to be the work of William Carver of Ripon . . .

Wind shook the leaded glass; Rod longed to be back at Thornton, having tea in the warm kitchen. He hurried through the village. His anorak had a slit in the shoulder and a cold wet patch was spreading. His shoulders hunched, he started to jog. Six racehorses went past him; Nora had said this part of Yorkshire was full of racing stables. Perched high, the stable boys looked haughtily down at him; a horse dropped a steaming pile of dung near his feet. Behind him, unseen by him, the afternoon bus from Ripon deposited Claudia in the market place.

Nora was carefully printing JAMES DILKS ELSTED HOUSE SCHOOL into a shiny pair of black wellington boots as they lay on their sides on the kitchen table. There was a large brown pot of tea beside her.

'Help yourself, love. The boys aren't back yet.' She dragged on her cigarette before going back to the boots. 'My Jimmy put a spike right through his other pair.' She sighed.

Rod poured himself a mug, and sat on the table. The kitchen was warm and dry, and whatever was cooking smelt good. Nora chatted easily to him; she was one of those rare people

14

who were never at a loss for words in whatever company, and yet whose need to communicate was matched by an ability to listen.

'What do you do for the rest of the year, Nora?'

'I'm a matron at this prep school down in Cheshire.' She pointed to the words Elsted House. 'Jimmy goes to the school at a special rate, so I'm lucky. Being a single parent can have its problems.' She put the boots on the floor. 'I didn't have much of an education. At least Jimmy's going to. Where do you go to school?'

'A local comprehensive. Quite good. I've left now—I'm going to university if my exam grades are good enough.'

'Claudia was saying hers were due soon.'

'Too soon. Nerve-racking.'

'Did you like your comprehensive? I mean, there are big public schools in London, aren't there? St Paul's and that? Didn't you want to go to them?'

'My parents chose the state system.'

'But did you go along with that? I mean, some think the public schools are best.'

'Nora. I'm surprised at you, really I am.' Dick came into the kitchen. 'What heresies am I hearing now?'

'It's a free country. I can ask Rod what he thinks, can't I?'

'I'm not sure what I think—' Rod began.

'Well, you can be sure if all the independent schools were abolished tomorrow, our state system would be the best in the world.' Dick could talk about education for hours. Nora pushed back her chair.

'Let me tell you I'm bloody glad Jimmy's not in a state school any more. Our little set-up suits us a treat.' She moved her packet of cigarettes away from Dick's exploring fingers. 'Hands off. You buy your own, mate.'

'Aw, come on Nora, just one—'

'No. It's always just one. You left-wing types are all the same, the biggest cadgers in the business. Full of theories about the bright world of the future, and in debt to the present.'

15

'What have I done to deserve this vitriol—'

'I'm broke this week. It puts me in a bad mood. I had to get Jimmy a new pair of wellies and it upset my budget.' She buttoned her packet away in the top pocket of the old bush jacket she was wearing. Her clothes were a graceless mixture of colours and styles; she clearly had no interest whatever in her appearance.

Dick hardly listened to her explanation. 'It's people like you, Nora, who undermine what the education authorities are trying to do—'

'Fill up my mug for me, Rod, there's a love. I don't mind it strong.'

'It's really orange now.'

'Suits me.'

'Don't you see what I mean, Nora—'

'Look, Dick, I live my life the best I can, and go for quality where I can find it. I've got no theories. A school's a school: if it teaches well, it's good, if it doesn't, it's bad. As far as I'm concerned that's all there is to it.'

'That's a theory in itself.'

'So what?'

'Argue with a woman and all you get is irrational prejudice.'

'Don't argue with them then. Not that you're right. I always find men are more prejudiced than women.' She opened her pocket and took out her cigarettes again. 'Tell you what, Dick, if I give you a fag will you leave off the subject of education?'

'You are a hopeless woman, Nora. I give up.' Dick paced over to the window and gazed out at the hillside.

'Have the fag anyway.' She coughed, and smiled at Rod. 'They say we smoke more up in the North.'

There was a pause while Dick got over his irritation at being prevented from having a discussion, but within minutes he was cheerful again as he outlined his plans for the evening and the next day. Rod began to see how good Dick was at his job; his enthusiasm was endless.

Unmistakable sounds from the hall indicated that the boys

16

were back. The roar spread throughout the house. Nora hurried off to stop muddy boots from being taken upstairs; Kevin passed her as she left the kitchen. He went over to the teapot and poured half an inch of tea into a mug. 'Disgusting.' He threw the dregs into the sink and filled his mug with cold water instead. Having drunk this, he went out again.

'Charming fellow, our Kevin. So open and friendly.' Dick took all the mugs over to the sink and rinsed them.

'He never meets your eyes.'

'He does when he's angry. Then it's like being on the receiving end of a blowlamp.' Dick wiped down the table with the practised movements of someone used to housework. 'Our Kevin fancies Claudia.'

'Oh. And Claudia? I can't see her liking him.' Rod kept his voice light, as did Dick.

'You never know with Claudia. She likes to keep her options open.' He rubbed again vigorously at the clean table. 'She's a devil, that girl.'

A devil I can't wait to see again. But all Rod said out loud was: 'See you later.'

Why did I go to Ripon, why? Stupid, stupid me. I knew it would go wrong. When he didn't ring me back, I knew it. I should have stayed at home, but instead I go and hang about and waste my time because he's too busy to see me. And he's furious with me for bothering him . . . Why did I go? You're a silly cow, Claudia Dalton, you ought to learn the art of playing it cool.

I swear this hill has got longer in the night. The ride is killing me this morning. And I'm late. Oh, to get off my bike and go to sleep in the hedge; one of these days I will and to hell with them all. Except that I know I would dream of Nora slaving away . . . wouldn't it be lovely not to have a conscience.

2

There she was, behind the hatch at breakfast. Overcome with nerves, beaming, Rod stammered good morning. She looked tired and sullen, and hardly acknowledged his greeting. She was wearing a large, bright yellow jersey which made her face look sallow, purple jeans, and had twisted her long hair in a viciously tight knot on top of her head. She hardly resembled the irresponsible extrovert of two days ago with a cloud of brown hair merging into a simple cotton dress. She grunted when Rod asked her if she'd had a good day off. From behind him, Dick said:

'It looks as if it was a hard day's night.'

'Piss off.'

Claudia left the hatch taking with her the empty scrambled-egg saucepan; Nora took over and winked at the boys.

'Claudie love, bring over another tray of rolls. And mind your language.'

The bangs and clatters from the kitchen were louder than usual throughout the meal, and, when Claudia came in to clear the tables just as Dick and Rod were finishing, she continued her work noisily. As she stacked plates she suddenly said:

'I hear we have a new star in our midst. Rod the Rocker, heart-throb of the dollies of the Dales.'

'Don't mock. He's very good. You haven't heard him.' Dick got up and hurried out, clipboard in hand.

'I'm not good, I'm average. No more.'

'Modesty will get you nowhere.'

'I don't want to get anywhere.'

Claudia took a loaded tray to the hatch and slid it through.

19

'Do you play classical guitar, or just folk?'

'Both.'

She began to wipe down the pale blue formica tables with long rhythmic strokes. As she leant over near him, Rod felt an almost uncontrollable desire to put his hands on her slim purple hips. He piled his plates up quickly.

'Don't hurry because of me. I'll do your table last.'

'I've finished.' The dining room seemed very empty and private. 'Can I help?'

'No, it's O.K.' Claudia pushed chairs straight, before she said offhandedly: 'Next time you play, let me know and I'll come and listen.'

'If you know anything about the guitar, you won't enjoy it much.'

Claudia faced him. The black make-up round her eyes was smudged, and her hair was coming down from its knot in wisps on her neck. She grinned; her face seemed all grin and eyes. 'I like all sorts of rubbish. I'm not fussy.' She raised her hand, as if dismissing him, and Rod smiled back and made for the door.

As he came out of the dining room, Kevin passed him. 'There's no one in there except Claudia,' he began, but Kevin did not stop. He shut the dining room door firmly behind him. Rod stood nearby, upset by the thought that Kevin and Claudia had anything to say to each other. He hung about for five minutes but Kevin did not reappear. Dick then dragged him off to play volleyball with the boys.

When he saw Claudia at teatime she beckoned him over; she was doing a crossword. 'Rod, let me pick your brains. Everyone else has failed me. "Places of amusement provide loud music"? Five letters, third one I.'

'Disco—no, silly, it's a plural word to start with—dives—I keep getting the I in the wrong place. *Fairs*.'

'That's it. That's it. Lovely. Clever old you.'

Rod sat down beside her, and they continued to solve the crossword at speed.

'Hey, we're a great team. We ought to do it first thing in the morning and send it in. We might win a prize.' Claudia surveyed the almost finished crossword with pleasure.

'Hardly worth the slog for a quid.' Dick could not do crosswords.

'They pay three now.'

'Ten down is "sadist".'

'Right. Two more to go—what about sixteen across?'

'I'm stuck on that one.' Claudia's head was very close to his; more of her hair had escaped from its knot and lay against her cheek and neck in curling fronds. His breath moved those nearest to him. Claudia suddenly pushed the newspaper away, and stood up. 'I'm for a walk before the rush starts again. Who'll come? Dick? Kevin?'

To Rod's delight only he was interested, and they set off together towards the gate at the back of the house which gave onto a track going straight up the moor. The ground was very wet from the rain of the day before, and little streams, half underground, gurgled on all sides. Claudia led the way over a stile built into a drystone wall, and they moved from half-cultivated fields to rough, tussocky moorland.

'I love these moors. I've lived here for ten years and I never get tired of them. I love their shape, their smell, their colours.'

'Where did you live before?'

'Near Birmingham.' Claudia walked fast up the indistinct path; for twenty minutes they climbed in silence until they reached the vantage point she had been aiming for. She lay down on the springy turf as Rod looked about him. Down the dale beyond Thornton he could see the river winding out of sight, a golden twisting strip with the sun dropping beyond it. The moors behind him and across the valley were between one and two thousand feet high, and the late afternoon light gave them extra colour: purple, dark green, browns of every tone. Narrow crooked valleys bit into the hillsides, and in many huddled rowan trees, their berries a piercing scarlet. The neat drystone walls ran like partings across the lower moors, friendly and domestic; beyond them the high moors were less tamed. Sheep bleated all round, a sound that would have been melancholy if it had not been so mindless. Rod stretched as he looked at the view.

'Fantastic, isn't it.' Claudia lay with her eyes wide open, staring past him into the sky. 'This is the best time of day. I often come here.'

'The moors are better than I expected. I always thought they were an apology for real mountains.'

'What blasphemy. They're better than mountains to me. Yet some people don't like them. Nora's one. She says they make her feel redundant; she prefers flatter country where she can see round corners, she says. Funny Nora. Nothing will make her come up here.'

'I like them.'

Claudia had crawled over to some small untidy bushes and was searching under their reddish leaves. 'Bilberries. They are the most elusive little beggars.' She picked a small berry and ate it; it left a purple stain on her lip. Rod found he kept looking at this stain.

'Does Kevin like moors?'

'No idea.' Claudia wriggled over to another clump of bilberries. 'He walks over them a lot, but then he's a fitness freak.' She stood up, handing Rod a bilberry. 'Try it.'

It was sweet, unusual, rather pippy; Claudia laughed at his expression. 'They're an acquired taste.'

'I wouldn't have known they were edible.'

'Londoner.'

'So what.'

'What part of London do you live in?'

'The south. Sydenham.'

'I don't know the south at all. I've cousins who live in Highgate. I stay with them occasionally.' She spoke dreamily. 'But I intend to live in London myself one day, when I'm studying.'

'Studying what?'

Claudia did not answer; Rod wondered if she had heard. He was about to repeat the question, when she surprised him.

'You have a shadow in your heart, Rod—Rod what, by the way?'

He swallowed. 'Parrish.'

'My surname's Dalton. I can sense a pain or something sitting inside you like a toad.'

Rod stared at her in silence for a moment, and then was about to pour out everything, his father's attempted suicide, the misery at home—but she went on, unaware, 'Don't worry, I won't ask what it is. I just wanted to tell you I knew it was there. Sometimes it's a help if someone else knows.' She got up as she spoke. 'I must go. I heard the church clock strike the half hour some time ago—it must be getting on for six. You stay. You're in no hurry, after all.' She bounced away down the hill at great speed, her yellow and purple clothes bright against the dun colours.

The moor was very still. There was almost no wind, and apart from the sheep and the chirping of little birds Rod later discovered were pippits, no sound either. He flung himself down on the turf where Claudia had lain. A shadow inside him like a toad: it did somehow feel like that. A cold unpleasant toad. But how had she known? If only she hadn't gone; he longed to tell her all about it. That was a way of banishing the toad, he was sure.

He sat up. He was beginning to find the solitude intimidating. He tried to relax, gazing at the view; clouds now covered the sun, and it was chilly. The minutes crawled by. He made himself stay longer, still hoping that his loneliness would turn into a more productive state of mind. The church clock in Thornton struck six; he got up and began to return to the house, depressed at his lack of inner strength.

He hoped to catch Claudia after supper, but she left immediately the washing up was done. Rod had to help with this in the evenings, and was beginning to like the fact his duties took him into the kitchen. He was about to suggest some coffee

23

to Claudia, when she said briskly:

'I'm off, Nora. What was it you wanted me to bring up?'

'Scourers and lavatory cleaner.'

'Right. See all you good people tomorrow.'

Claudia took her old bike out of the back porch and rode off through the half-dark. Rod, leaning on the kitchen window sill, watched her go. As her yellow jersey disappeared through the trees, he could feel dejection spreading through him.

'Come and have coffee with me in my little sitting room.' Nora spoke gently behind him. 'That is, if you haven't anything better to do.'

'Thanks, Nora. I will.' He followed her up a steep flight of back stairs to a small untidy room above the kitchen. It had a notice on the door saying 'Housekeeper's Office'. Nora put a glass coffee-maker on an electric ring.

'I like proper coffee sometimes. Wish I could afford it every day. Take a seat.'

There were two tattered old armchairs, a large basket full of mending, an ironing board which Nora fixed at its lowest to serve as a coffee table, and little else. One wall of the room was all cupboards, containing the household linen.

Nora sat down beside the mending basket. 'I'm going to have a fag before I even look at that lot.' She pushed it aside with her foot.

Rod took the chair by the window. Far away down the long drive through the dark shafts of trees bobbed Claudia's yellow jersey. The drive was full of mud-filled ruts, and she was clearly swerving from left to right to avoid them.

'There goes Claudia.'

'That girl's a baggage. A nice baggage, but a baggage. All men like Claudia. She never makes the slightest effort to attract them, which is no doubt why they can't resist her.'

All talk about Claudia affected Rod deeply; he found it impossible to be objective. It was galling to find his feelings for Claudia so widely shared. The yellow jersey disappeared out of the main gates; Rod turned as Nora handed him a mug of

24

coffee.

'Sugar? Help yourself. Beware of Claudia, Rod; she can hurt people.'

'We all can.'

'Claudia's better at it than most. People misunderstand her—they think she's a special friend and then they discover she treats everyone the same. Then they're jealous.'

Rod did not answer. He began to wonder whether it was Nora who was jealous of Claudia's youth.

'Never mind Claudia. Tell me about yourself, and your family. Sisters? Brothers?'

'Two sisters, Julia who's seventeen, a year younger than me, Lucy who's fifteen.'

'No brothers? And what does your Dad do?'

'He's a civil servant. Used to be a teacher.' The toad jumped inside him, hurting. There was a silence. Nora had asked all the polite questions; she moved restlessly in her chair, tapping off her ash. Suddenly Rod went on:

'We had a dreadful family crisis a couple of months ago. He tried to commit suicide. Julia and I found him before it was too late.' There, he had told someone. He wished it had been Claudia, but Nora would do.

'Your poor family.' She gazed at him in concern. 'What a shock. Is everything all right now?'

'Seems to be. How can one tell?'

'You're right. You just have to have faith.' Nora put her empty mug down and picked up some sewing. 'I don't know how a family copes with a situation like that, I really don't.'

'It's the aftermath that's worst.' Rod ran a thumbnail over the design of red flowers round his mug. 'You can't stop thinking about why he did it. It sort of poisons you.'

'You mustn't let it.'

'I didn't at first. But recently I've begun to realize the whole thing was probably my fault.'

'Rod. I know nothing about what happened, but I would guess it's nobody's fault. People act for such a mixture of reasons at the best of times. Would you say this wool was dark blue or black?'

'Er, black. There's always such tension between me and my father. We've never got on. He's very possessive and I've fought against it all my life.'

'That's a familiar story, you know. It doesn't usually bring about such terrible results. Does your father suffer from mental illness at all? That would be much more likely to push him over the brink than anything you could do or say.'

Rod could hear Dick calling him down in the kitchen. 'He does suffer from acute depressions.'

'There you are then.'

'He wasn't depressed when it happened.'

Dick called again, and Rod stood up. Nora took his hand. 'I always feel that people are like icebergs, most of what is going on in their lives and heads is always invisible.'

'Is Rod up there, Nora?'

'Just coming. Thanks for the coffee, Nora. And the sympathy.'

'Don't let what your Dad did poison you any more. You must put it behind you.'

Rod hesitated inside the door. 'This afternoon when we were walking up on the moor, Claudia suddenly said out of the blue: you've got a shadow in your heart. I hadn't told her anything about it.'

'Well, you banish that shadow.'

'I'll try. But how strange Claudia sensed it.'

Nora's head was bent over the sock she was mending. 'When all's said and done, Claudia's special. I admit it. I freely admit it.'

'Thanks again for the coffee.'

Oh despair, despair. How I hate this work. But I need the money, I need the money. No one else is going to pay for my dream to come true. It's a mad dream, but never mind. Madder dreams have succeeded. Aim for the stars, girl, even if you miss them . . .

I like Rod, I'm glad he's come. Perhaps a bit of competition from him will stop Kevin breathing down my neck. Not that I mind Kevin, the silent edgy type is attractive. Rod's not bad either—he's got a sort of secret strength. And the best smile you can imagine. I just wish Nora would stop nagging at me; it's not my fault the boys get interested in me. I don't particularly want them to be.

Unlike Gerry. I'd love him to be exclusively, passionately interested in little me—instead I know I'm one of a herd of women chasing after him. The competition's so heavy I can't hope to win. But he does care, I know he does. He's even said he does, after all. He wouldn't spend any time at all with me if he didn't. Then he ignores me for weeks on end. Oh Gerry, Gerry. Damn you. I sometimes wish you didn't exist.

'Claudia, have you finished the staircase yet?'
'Nearly.'
'I'll make the coffee then.'
'Great, Nora, I need it.' *To soothe my battered heart . . .*

3

As Rod took the boys through a folk song, Claudia slipped into the room and sat in a corner. She was drinking a mug of coffee. The boys rustled and grinned at her.

'It's no good trying to be inconspicuous. Come and join in.' Rod handed her a copy of the words; he had scrawled them out making as many carbon copies as possible; this copy was nearly illegible. Claudia took it and leant on a table near him. She was wearing a baggy, blue cotton dress belted with plaited scarves; more scarves were round her neck, the ends trailing down her back. Her hair was loose today, thick and bouncy. After the harshness of her scraped-back style, this soft hair round her face made her look dreamily beautiful.

'Don't mind me,' she said.

Rod picked up his guitar again. How could he not mind her; his mind was full of her. He played his guitar badly until his fingers recovered from the effect of her arrival. Then he asked her if there was anything she'd like to have them sing.

'Well, let's stick to folk. Do you know *Donna, Donna*?'

'The tune, not the words.' He played chords and hummed.

'I know all the words.' There was a blackboard propped against the wall; in a firm sweeping hand she wrote the chorus on it:

How the winds are laughing
They laugh with all their might
Laugh and laugh the whole day through
And half the summer night.
Donna, donna, donna etc.

She turned to the boys. 'If you all sing that chorus like mad, I'll

28

sing the verses. Is that all right, Rod?'

'Fine.'

The boys had all watched her as she wrote with close and elbow-nudging attention. They now gazed at her in open anticipation.

'Right, boys. Once through the chorus with me.' She sang it slowly and they tried to follow her. She took them through it again. 'Much better. O.K., maestro? Give me a few chords' introduction.' Rod bowed, partly to mock her, but mainly to hide his eagerness to hear her sing alone.

'On a wagon bound for market
There's a calf with a mournful eye,
High above him there's a swallow
Winging swiftly through the sky.'

She sang commandingly, straight-backed, head up, in a clear, powerful voice. She achieved the sliding tones of a folk singer in her own peculiar way, her voice losing none of its ringing authority. Rod muffed several chords in his excitement at the sounds she made. Everyone joined enthusiastically in the chorus, and she went on:

'"Stop complaining," said the farmer,
"Who told you a calf to be,
Why don't you have wings to fly with
Like the swallow so proud and free?"

'Calves are easily bound and slaughtered,
Never knowing the reason why,
But whoever treasures freedom
Like the swallow has learned to fly.'

After the final chorus there were claps and shouts for more. Claudia laughed. She was clearly a seasoned performer, and went straight into *It takes a worried man to sing a worried song*, which the boys knew and joined in noisily. At the end of it Claudia said:

'I must go—end of coffee break. Now where's my mug?' A scramble of boys leapt at it, with the result that it fell and

29

broke. 'Never mind.' She heard Nora shouting her name, and hurried out.

Rod tried to do more with the boys, but failed; they were infected with restless euphoria and he told them to go and run it off in the grounds. Left in the silence, he began to collect up the word-sheets. Claudia's voice amazed him; he must find out how she came to sing like that. He dumped his guitar against the staircase, and went on to the kitchen to ask her, but she waved him away.

'Out,' said Nora. 'We're busy.'

'Come on, Claudia, people don't sing like that just from practising in the bath.'

'Secret.' She laughed again.

'Out, I said, or you'll get no lunch.' Nora shut the door firmly.

All day Rod tried to catch Claudia, but she was busily elusive. After tea he looked for her in case she wanted a walk up the moor; he decided, when he couldn't find her, that she had probably gone up there already. He walked up by himself, sure he would find her, rehearsing in his mind what they might say to each other.

But the moor was empty. He stood on the level place Claudia had showed him and felt utterly dejected. As he gazed absent-mindedly down at the house wondering what to do next, he suddenly saw, his gaze sharpening, Claudia playing tennis with Kevin on the court beyond the games pitch. She had tucked her long blue dress up short, and her strong white legs looked unnaturally long as she ran barefoot round the court. Rod was consumed with purest jealousy of Kevin. Neither of them played well; he could hear Claudia's laughter as she hit a particularly high lob well out of court.

Unable to watch any more, Rod turned and walked further up the moor until King's Thornton was out of sight. At the top of a secondary valley, he came upon a collection of derelict stone buildings, a lead mine, though he did not know it. These ruins, despite their isolation, were not melancholy; there was a settled rounded quality about them that was comforting. Sheep bounded out of one half-doorway, bleating in alarm. Rod sat for some time against a wall, so still that the sheep returned and cropped the turf quite near him.

'Fetch the meat for me, Rod, there's a love. The butcher rang to say his van's broken down.'

'Oh. Yes, O.K. I'm free till ten thirty.'

'Yes, I know, Dick said. Claudia's down in the village, but I can't get hold of her. No reply from her place at all. Otherwise she could have fetched it up.' Nora yawned.

'No, no, I'll go. It won't take me any time.'

'If you see Claudia tell her to get a move on. Dratted girl.' Nora yawned again. 'I sleep badly in this place, can't think why.'

Rod took an empty knapsack and hurried down to the village. He would find Claudia and walk back with her. The desire to see her alone, to talk to her, was so strong, he would have carried a hundredweight of meat for miles.

He was told at the butcher's to wait, as the parcels of meat had not yet been retrieved from the broken-down van, but someone was on their way to it now in a car . . . Rod wandered out, and casually searched the village for a sign of Claudia. He could ask the butcher where Claudia Dalton lived, but decided it wasn't worth it.

He wandered into the churchyard, where he had a surprise. Tucked in the church porch was Claudia's bicycle, unmistakable because of a green-painted basket with C D in white on the front. Delighted to have tracked her down, he pushed the heavy main door open, and was inside the church before he realized there was a service going on. He stopped awkwardly. There were half a dozen people up near the altar, and the wild-headed man he had seen on his previous visit was standing before it in rich green vestments. On his left knelt a long-haired boy in a white surplice. It was only when the boy lifted his face and turned slightly that Rod realized it was not a boy at all, but Claudia. Shaken, he backed quickly out of the church, hoping she had not seen him. He collected the meat and trudged back up the hill, still unnerved by the unexpected sight of Claudia kneeling at the altar. He had just reached King's Thornton gates twenty minutes later, when he heard a bicycle bell ringing insistently behind him. He turned, and saw Claudia waving as she pedalled uphill.

'Hi. Saw you stagger out of church.' She chuckled as she jumped off her bicycle.

'I—I didn't know there was a service going on. I came to look at the misericords.'

'You should have waited. My father doesn't bite.'

'Your father . . .'

'Henry Dalton—the vicar.' She laughed at Rod's expression. 'Didn't you know?'

'No one told me.'

'I serve for Dad occasionally in the holidays. He likes us to do it, but my sisters won't. So I do it.'

Claudia scooted her bike beside Rod as he strode quickly along. 'That knapsack looks heavy. Put it in my basket.'

'Oh. All right.' Rod eased the pack off, and the basket creaked under its weight. 'It's Nora's meat. The butcher's van broke down.'

'I could have saved you the bother—'

'She did try and contact you—'

They set off again in silence, Claudia riding slowly and Rod jogging. The house came into view; boys were milling round the front. Rod wanted to stop, to freeze his time with Claudia; there was so much he wanted to talk to her about. He wanted to know the whole of her life, to tell her the whole of his. 'Please come for a walk today,' he burst out.

'Why not? Why not. I'll meet you at half past four at the back gate.' She swerved away towards the back door. 'Don't bother, I'll give the meat to Nora.' Rod jumped backwards and for-wards over a low wall as he ran towards the house, whistling in his delight. He then took the boys down to the games pitch and organized football with great vigour. The boys really were an extremely nice lot, he decided.

At precisely half past four Rod sat on the gate waiting. Ten minutes went by, then he heard voices and footsteps. Claudia appeared with Dick in tow. Rod scowled at him.

'Look, I arranged with Claudia this morning—'

'She invited me,' protested Dick. 'But what the hell. I know when I'm not wanted.' He left quickly, despite Claudia calling after him.

'Now look Rod, that was mean—'

'I don't want to go for a walk with Dick. I've been with him most of the day—'

'I asked him because he looked miserable. Now he'll be even more miserable.'

'He'll survive.'

'I can't stand possessive males.'

'I wasn't being possessive.'

'You could have fooled me.'

'Shall I run after dear Dick then, and force him to join us?'

'Don't be silly, Rod. Let's go for this walk; we've wasted enough time.' She swung herself neatly over the gate. 'Have you been down by the river bank? You cross by one plank and return lower down by another. It's a good walk.'

'Great.'

'You may not like the bridge.'

He did not like it. Two narrow planks spanned the stony river, with a slack wire as a handrail above them. Claudia walked unconcernedly across and Rod shuffled behind her. He had a bad sense of balance and no head for heights. When he finally caught up with her she was singing to herself.

'Tell me how you learned to sing so well.'

'I just sing.' She did not look at him.

'But you know what you're doing—do you sing with a choir or group?'

'I belong to the Folk Club at school, not that it's much good.

I learn songs off records, copy the singer's style if I like it.'

'You sang so well yesterday. You really have a good voice. I mean it.'

She turned and met his glance; there was a serious look in her eye as if she was assessing something. 'Do you know anything about singing?'

'I know you're good.'

She turned away again. 'I sometimes sing at local hops where they need a cabaret – my sister Josephine plays the piano for me, and we're a crashing success. Naturally.' She laughed, and thwacked the undergrowth with a straight branch she had picked up. 'Our audience would like it whatever we did. No one could call them discriminating.' After a pause she added: 'It was nice to sing to a guitar.'

'Haven't you done that before?'

'Not often. The guitarists in the Folk Club are not nearly as good as you.'

'Come and do it again.'

'I might.'

'But your voice is really something special, Claudia.' She seemed to resist what he was saying; he had to make her see. 'Way beyond the ordinary. Has no one ever told you?'

'Anyone can sing as long as they're uninhibited enough.' She was smiling to herself, and he got the impression she did not believe what she said. Silence fell between them as they negotiated a gully full of nettles, brambles and bracken. Rod collected nettle stings all along one arm, and was rubbing dock leaves into them when Claudia said:

'Nora told me about your father's attempted suicide.'

'She had no business to tell you.' He dropped the crushed leaves. 'It was up to me to tell you. I was going to—'

'She meant well—'

'I wanted to tell you the other day up on the moor, but you rushed off before I could.'

'Never mind. I just wanted to say I'm sorry. It can't be easy to live with that.'

34

Beams of sunshine lit up the woods around them, highlighting Claudia's hair, cobwebs, the edges of leaves. 'I'm getting used to it. Coming north was a good idea.' The woodland ended for a space, and they waded through shoulder-high bracken. No undergrowth seemed impenetrable to Claudia: she never hesitated.

'You'd be good in a jungle.'

Claudia laughed.

'I can't believe you're a parson's daughter.'

'Don't be narrow-minded. Why should it make any difference?'

'I don't know—'

'People are so prejudiced about the priesthood—they can't seem to accept them as normal human beings. I don't mean just you, everyone's the same. My father says oh for the Middle Ages when being a religious was normal, natural and respected.'

'And celibate. No Claudias in the Middle Ages.'

Claudia laughed again. 'Except illegits. But seriously, do you know any priests?'

'No, not really.'

'Then you'd better come and meet one. My father's an old devil in many ways but everyone loves him.'

'Like you, perhaps.'

But Claudia walked quickly on, giving no indication she had heard Rod's softly spoken remark. They entered gnarled woodland, the bright green grass under the trees extending right to the water. Claudia suddenly grabbed his arm as both of them saw a bright flash of bluey green dart up the river. 'Kingfisher. Oh, fantastic. I haven't seen one for at least a year. Beloved, beautiful bird.' They stared at the busy river, but no blue flash reappeared. She said almost crossly to Rod: 'You don't know how lucky you are to see a kingfisher on your first walk.' Then she looked at his watch. 'Oh, hell. I'm going to be very late. Nora will not be pleased. I think it's quicker to turn back than go on. Do what you like, but I must hurry.'

35

'I'll come with you.' He followed her, still full of things to say to her. But she pressed on ahead, and the pace was too quick to allow for talking. Time had flown; it always flew when he was with Claudia. He longed for a satiety of her company. He saw her go lightly across the plank bridge, and shouted goodbye. She waved and disappeared through the trees on the opposite bank. Rod negotiated the unpleasant bridge at his own cowardly pace, pleased to be unobserved.

'You're a middle-class menace, Claudia.'

'So what?'

'So everything—what's wrong with this country is that the middle classes have run it for too long.'

'But Dick, tell me, am I a menace because I'm a menace or because I'm middle-class—'

'They have a stranglehold on it—'

'Is my menacedom personal or general?'

'It's the middle-class part of you I was referring to—'

'You've been brainwashed, Dick. Can't you see it? Class divisions are convenient umbrellas; what really matters is the unique individual. I'm me, my class is unimportant—'

'Claudia, I despair. You're only interested in your own little world, your own little self.'

'I'm *not*. I was giving "me" as an example. But I believe in the sanctity of the individual, and you don't. And yet you're kind and good—'

'It's hopeless, it's really hopeless.' Dick paced round the kitchen; Nora was peeling apples and Rod was sitting on the window sill listening while he untangled a long piece of string. 'Every discussion in this place turns into personal comment and gossip.' Dick took some apple peelings, and began to drop them into his mouth.

'You started it off by calling me a middle-class menace.'

'Only because you interrupted me with a really prejudiced remark—'

'I can't even remember what it was.' Claudia giggled. Dick

went up to her and shook her in mock rage.

'Just as well.' Nora sounded tired, even though she was smiling. 'Put some sugar on those apples, Claudia, will you, before they go brown.'

Kevin came in at that moment, holding some letters. He gave two to Nora and an official-looking card to Rod.

'God, not my results.' Rod shut his eyes. 'Look at it for me, Kevin.'

There was a pause before Kevin read out slowly. 'The following library books are overdue . . .'

Rod stood up on the window sill, clapping his hands and laughing in relief. 'This calls for more tea.' He leapt down. 'Do you mind, Nora?'

'Go ahead.' (Most of the time, Nora enjoyed having her kitchen used as a common room; every now and again, though, something would snap and she would shout with angry frustration and push them all out of the door.) She filled a large saucepan with apple and Claudia put it on the cooker to soften, stirring and prodding the fruit absent-mindedly. Rod stood beside her, watching the kettle. Claudia had streaks of flour on her face, and he wondered if he dared to brush them off. He longed to be easy and casual with Claudia, but she affected him so strongly that all spontaneity was stifled.

'Tennis, Claudia?' He heard Kevin's soft voice behind him.

'How lovely. Yes, I feel like belting the ball around.' Claudia turned as Kevin came up to her. He reached for a tea cloth and calmly wiped the flour off her face.

'Same time then.' He put the cloth over the back of a chair, and left the kitchen, ignoring Claudia's cry of, 'Don't you want any tea?'

'I don't think I do either.' Rod abandoned the kettle, and went outside, hating Kevin. It was a fine afternoon, but the sunshine oppressed him. Rod went back into the house and up the long main staircase to his room. The bare treads and echoing landings gave the house a desolate air; there were empty niches at regular intervals in the walls where once vases

37

and statues had stood. The dark mahogany banister rail was scarred and scratched in places. Rod saw some freshly cut initials, and bent in anger to examine them. Footsteps came lightly up the stairs below, and he heard Claudia call his name.

'I'm here. Next floor.'

'Don't come down—I'm coming up to the top floor; I have to get some blankets.' She joined him and they climbed together. The last flight to the attic floor was much narrower, and the banister rail was of pine. Claudia went into a cupboard, so large it was almost a room, and pulled out armfuls of blankets, saying as she did so:

'I thought you might like to come down and have supper with us one night.'

Rod was so taken aback he was silent.

'I know it's not a very exciting idea—'

'No, no, I'd love to. Thanks. Thanks.'

'Find out when Dick can best spare you. Saturday evening is a good one for my family.'

'I'll do my best to fix it for Saturday then.'

She went downstairs and Rod exploded into his room. He did three press-ups, a somersault and then lay on his bed and laughed. So she did like him a little; she had singled him out, asked him carefully in private. He lay thinking about Claudia, as he had never thought about a human being before. He was obsessed by her as he had once (not so long ago) been obsessed by motorbikes; he thought about her, was aware of her, schemed about her all his waking moments. But Claudia had the edge over his old bike; he laughed again. She had a heart. She did like him, he was sure of it.

He got up and leant out of his window. She was playing tennis with Kevin; he enjoyed the sight and shouted encouragement when she hit a good shot. She missed the next and smiling shook her fist at him. Kevin scowled in his direction.

Rod saw Dick wandering about below him. The boys were all on a coach outing, guided by a retired schoolmaster in the village who helped out each year in this way. Dick sat for a while on a wall finishing a cigarette, and then drifted towards the tennis players. His shoulders drooped, and he looked vulnerable and despondent. He sat by the court until Claudia suggested he played too.

'No racket.'

'Come on, Kevin, give Dick a turn.'

There was some discussion, and then Rod saw Kevin drop his racket and walk away. Dick, beaming, began to hit great looping lobs at Claudia.

Kevin walked away through trees until he was out of sight of the players. He stopped and stood still for a moment, and Rod saw that his expression was full of anguish.

Wednesday tomorrow, lovely Wednesday if I'm going to Ripon, dreary Wednesday if I'm not. Why isn't the horrible man ever in when I ring? And he never rings back, never. Perhaps they don't pass on the message. Then just when I've given up he rings at last, and has the cheek to say where have you been, what have you been up to?

'Ringing you, Gerry.'

'Sorry, sorry, life's been hectic. What were you ringing me about?'

Oh, what was I ringing you about—about everything, about nothing, about me and you, about the fact I love you too much—

'I was hoping to come to Ripon on Wednesday.' And then he says good, let's meet and have lunch, but sometimes he says Wednesday's no good, I can't. He never tells me why. That's when if I'm sensible I don't go to Ripon at all. If I'm sensible; am I ever sensible? I saw him once with that university lecturer friend of his, Angela someone, one of those elegant females who's got everything I haven't got plus maturity, and I felt so jealous I nearly died. I'd have been better off staying at home.

Which is a dead bore, because there's nothing else I want to do on my free day except go to Ripon to see Gerry. Mooching over to Richmond to go to the cinema is possible, but I know I'm just killing time. And if I stay at home the doorbell rings every five minutes, and it's old Mrs X who would like to see the dear Vicar, sorry he's out, never mind, when shall I call back to catch him, and as soon as she's gone the phone rings and it's the undertakers or some such, never a call for me.

What the hell. I'll ring him all evening until I get the sod; I'm determined to see him tomorrow.

4

Part of the front fence of the vicarage had been removed, and the garden was churned up with tyre tracks. Rod walked along the mangled path; to the right, about two hundred yards away, a new square brick house had been built and was at the point of completion. Posts for a fence had been staked round it, marking out a smallish portion of the large garden.

Ahead of Rod was an eighteenth-century country house with a central section and two wings, each one room deep. The wide front door had a damaged but beautiful fanlight over it, and the bell was a big white china knob in a dish of polished brass. The front steps were of worn York stone; the deep curves of wear looked oddly welcoming. As he rang the bell Rod could hear a piano.

'Hullo. You must be Rod. Come in, how nice to meet you. I'm Di Dalton, Claudia's mother.' She led Rod into a large, airy drawing room which took up the southern wing. It was full of battered furniture, and the polished floor had a few threadbare rugs on it. There was a grand piano in one corner, but the room was so big that the piano's own bulk was hardly noticeable. A girl was playing it; leaning on it was Claudia. The girl stopped when she saw Rod, and was introduced as Josephine.

'Don't let me stop you,' said Rod. Josephine flapped a hand in embarrassment, and eased herself out of the room. A smaller girl, Evelyn, bounced out of a chair and stared at him.

'My husband says please forgive him, he was called out suddenly, but he'll be back soon.'

'Have a sherry.' Claudia handed Rod a glass. She was offhand, and he felt his own delight at seeing her crumble inwardly.

'Thanks.'

'Or would you prefer a beer?' said Mrs Dalton.

'Well, yes—'

'Eve, fetch a big glass and a can from the fridge, darling, would you.'

Evelyn trailed unwillingly to the door. 'Can I have a Coke—'

'Oh, all right. Yes.'

Claudia plonked the sherry glass back on the mantelpiece, and stood gazing abstractedly at the recently lit log fire; the evening was just chilly enough to need it. There was a silence.

'You have a beautiful old house,' said Rod at last to Mrs Dalton.

'Only for a little while longer. Did you notice that red brick monstrosity in the corner of the garden?'

'The new house?'

'Our new home.' Claudia sighed audibly. Evelyn returned with Rod's beer, and when she heard what her mother was talking about, went out again. 'The powers-that-be have decided this house is far too large to be economic—'

'Which is true—' Claudia poked a log.

'—too large, and so they have built us a modern box, full of mod. cons. A housewife's dream, they hope. Thornton Vicarage will be sold to someone delighted with its perfect proportions, and we'll have to cram ourselves into rooms whose lack of symmetry will no doubt stunt our souls.' She laughed, her eyes glittering.

'Ma, it's pointless going on like this. You'll bore poor Rod stiff.'

'Yes, Rod, I'm sorry. It's just that as the moment draws nearer to leave this dear house, I'm getting increasingly upset about it. I thought I'd be resigned by now. I'm not.'

'Dad is.'

'Henry's completely blind to his surroundings.' Di Dalton took a mouthful of her sherry, and watched Claudia as she crossed to the big windows and closed the shutters noisily. 'I

42

shall miss all those shutters. There isn't a curtain in this house except in the attic rooms. And do you know, on the inside of one of the shutters upstairs is carved: "Good house, you are done", followed by several sets of initials and the date 1781. Very touching.'

'At least they aren't demolishing the house.'

'They can't, Rod. It's a listed building. Otherwise no doubt they would. I sometimes think the Church Commissioners are a lot of commercially-minded philistines.'

'Di, Di,' said a voice in the doorway, 'you are being unfair.'

'Change the subject, Dad, for goodness' sake,' muttered Claudia. She cast Rod a despairing glance.

Into the room came the wild-headed man; Rod immediately saw how alike father and daughter were. They both had the same forceful dark eyes, the same air of moody changeability. Henry Dalton shook hands firmly with Rod.

'How nice to meet another of the helpers. We liked Dick and Kevin. Loquacious Dick and silent Kevin—Claudia invited them together. I told her she shouldn't have done that—perhaps Kevin would have talked to us if he'd come on his own.' While he talked, he removed his detachable dog-collar and dropped it on the mantelpiece. As he loosened his top button he said to Rod: 'I apologize for being late and for my working clothes.'

'Kevin never talks much.' Claudia's humour had improved with the arrival of her father. 'He conducts his whole life with the absolute minimum of words.'

'It's disconcerting for the rest of us.' Rod folded himself into a chair full of lumpy springs. 'We then all talk too much as a sort of nervous reaction.'

Claudia laughed. 'It isn't nervous reaction with Dick; it's necessity.'

'Tell me about yourself, and how you like King's Thornton.' Henry Dalton's bright eyes invited Rod with genuine interest. Rod began to talk freely as he never had done before in Claudia's presence. His feelings about her had always inhibited

43

him; now he talked ostensibly to her father but aware of her attention he opened out and became his natural self. By the time they went into the kitchen to eat a very good meal, Rod could not remember being happier. After supper he helped them all wash up, and although Claudia hardly talked to him, her glance was warm, and he enjoyed working at her side.

Hanging high against the kitchen ceiling was an old-fashioned clothes dryer, neatly festooned with clothes of all colours and shapes. Rod was very tall and every time he crossed to the dresser with plates, he had to dodge dangling trouser legs. He recognized Claudia's purple trousers. He thought of Claudia inside them, and dropped two of the knives he was drying. The clothes drew his eye irresistibly: he saw small collapsed garments which he knew stretched on wear into bikini briefs; he saw bras and petticoats.

'Ma, your standards are slipping. I've just realized we've entertained our honoured guest with our washing still festooned about.' Claudia's tone was dry.

'Oh well. As the move gets nearer, I seem to get more and more disorganized. I feel as if I'm hypnotized by some horrid snake; I feel inert and powerless.' Di tipped dirty water down the sink and turned to dry her hands.

'Forbidden subject,' said Claudia.

Henry stood hovering by the back door. 'I'm just going over to the church for a moment to prepare things for tomorrow. Would you like to come and see it? It's a famous Yorkshire church.'

'I've had a quick look—' Rod glanced at Claudia. He only wanted to go if she came too. But she avoided his eyes, and went out of the kitchen shouting for Josephine. He swallowed. 'Of course I'd like to come. Places look different at night.'

Rod followed Henry out of the back door. They went down a path and through a small archway in the garden wall; it held a fine wrought-iron gate which gave a piercing squeak as they opened it.

The church roof shone almost white in the moonlight. Rod

followed Henry into the pitch dark building as the clock above them struck ten. With a practised series of flicks Henry switched on all the lights, and then left Rod while he went into the vestry. Rod wandered disconsolately up the church; every minute here was time stolen from Claudia's company. He lifted up a misericord: there was the pig with a bagpipe and dancing piglets. The pig had a robust, amiable expression; the two piglets were leaping high in their glee, their little trotters poised for eternal action. Rod ran his hand over them and could not help smiling. He looked at another seat, the one with the monk at the door of his cell. It was like seeing the face of a friend again, the wooden features were so full of expression. Henry came up behind him.

'Lord God, pity me: my infancy was stupid,
    my boyhood vain, my adolescence unclean.
But now, Lord Jesus, my heart has been
    set on fire with holy love . . .
See, I am dying through love!
Come down, Lord.
Come, Beloved, and ease my longing
See how I love, I sing, I glow, I burn.'

Rod remained crouching as Henry recited these words sonorously into the echoing church.

'That's a carving of Richard Rolle, who wrote those words in his most famous work, *The Fire of Love.*'

'Ah.'

Henry moved off to finish his preparations, and Rod stayed in his crouched position. *See how I love, I sing, I glow, I burn* . . . Oh, Claudia. He could no longer see the wooden monk, he could see only Claudia's white freckled face and vivid eyes, her wide mouth, her thick hair which she sometimes dealt with so severely—oh Claudia. *See, I am dying through love* . . .

Henry shut the vestry door. Rod hurried to the back to join him; he could not wait to get back to the house and Claudia. He was afraid Henry might take him on a detailed guided tour round the church, but to his relief the priest switched off the lights and locked up the building. As he did so, he talked.

'For years, I have been working on a biography of Rolle. As my family will tell you, he's my main obsession in life. The research has been easy, it's the writing the book which has been my problem. I can write a sermon, but anything longer—a total block sets in. Words slip, slide, congeal, escape . . .'

Rod was only half-listening to him as they walked back to the house. The crunch of their soles, the screech of a little owl, the creaking of old trees above them were more immediate than the literary problems of his host.

'And another difficulty is the depiction of a saintly man . . . how can one capture godliness, goodness, in words? . . .'

Rod stared at the moonlit garden. He had never seen his surroundings with this clarity. The little blades of grass at the edge of the path, the dandelions and daisies with closed heads, the etched beauty of the gravel . . .

'And so for nine years I have fought with Rolle's shadow, listing facts and figures and theories, but never writing anything in my own words that I felt captured his essence . . . Ah well.'

Through the windows came the sound of Claudia singing, the same song about the calf going to market. The piano limped behind her. Rod's awareness of the garden ebbed away, and he blinked.

'Claudia has a very good voice.'

'Has she? Perhaps it's familiarity, but I don't care much for the noise she makes. She also has rather a small repertoire, which tends to get irritating. But then I'm not in the least musical. Di is more so.'

As they entered the house Claudia stopped singing in mid-phrase and began an argument with her sister about the accompaniment. 'Either you come in too late or you hurry me—'

'Well, I hate accompanying anyway. You keep changing the tempo.' Josephine banged down the piano lid. 'I don't want to do this cabaret.'

'They're going to pay us, Jo. I've made the agreement now.'

Claudia saw her father in the doorway. 'Dad, make her see sense. She's being hopeless about it. We can't let them down now. Anyway, I want to do it.'

'We'll make fools of ourselves in front of all those people—'

'You'll know lots of them—'

'That makes it worse.'

'You managed perfectly well at the last barn dance; everyone said how good they thought we were together—'

'A captive audience of biased parishioners—'

Henry ignored his daughters' argument, and drifted away to his study. Claudia looked gloomily at Rod; Jo sulked. Suddenly Claudia smiled. 'Rod. Your guitar. You could accompany on your guitar. Let me explain. The local Antiquarian Society (Dad's chairman) is holding a fund-raising dance, and they asked me to provide a cabaret. Now Jo has got cold feet—'

'I'd much rather someone else did it—'

'I'd love to.' Rod was so fervent Claudia looked momentarily uneasy.

'Great. It's in a couple of weeks' time, just about when the summer session ends at King's Thornton.'

'So we'll have time to rehearse.'

'Yeah. I'll give you a list of the songs I know, and we can cook up a programme lasting about twenty minutes.'

'Shall we have a look at your songs now?'

'No.' Claudia yawned, showing white even teeth in her broad mouth. 'Sorry, but I'm flaked. All this getting up at six-thirty finishes me off.'

'I'm going to bed.' Josephine raised a hand in Rod's direction and went upstairs. Claudia yawned again, and flopped down into a sofa.

'Ma gets livid because I fall asleep on this and here I am hours later. She has a sixth sense about us all being in bed or not and she comes down and brutally wakes me. Oh, cruel, cruel mother.' She smiled to herself, her eyes closed.

'Our rock band often did small gigs and concerts, so I've

had a little experience . . .'

'Um. Good.' She chuckled, her eyes still closed. 'Certainly more than I have.'

As Rod walked back up to King's Thornton his mood of elation stayed with him. The moon was almost full, and the moors above him were ashen grey cut with the black shadows of valleys. He decided to walk up there now, and skirting the big house joined the path to the moor. The moonlight made dips and hillocks deceptive and he tripped frequently. He had to use all his attention to keep on his feet. When he reached Claudia's ridge, he turned and looked down at the darkened valley. King's Thornton had no lights on; in the village beyond there were only a few. He stared at the moors around him, at the clear black sky and the orb of the moon. *I love, I sing, I glow, I burn* . . . A divine creator was a distinct possibility. Rod shut his eyes, seeing two silver discs against the flesh of his lids. A distinct possibility . . .

Then he shivered. A wind was rising, and a thick band of high cloud was slowly approaching the moon. It would cut most of the light. Rod began to hurry down the moor. He had no idea what the time was. He had no key to the house, he realized; he hoped the kitchen door had been left open. But it was locked, as was every door he tried. Dick was obsessive about locking up.

Silence and darkness. The silence was shattered as Rod knocked over a stack of flowerpots and grazed his shin in the process. He waited, sure that the noise would disturb either Dick or Nora. But there was no reaction from the house so he began a despairing search for an open window. There was only the ground-floor lavatory window. It was a tight squeeze; he tore his pocket on the catch as he went head first, bearing down on the lavatory cistern. A tin of Vim fell with a clatter on the floor. He cursed as white powder shot out. While he was closing the window, a nervous voice on the other side of the door said:

48

'Who is it? What's going on?'

Rod flung the door open and saw Dick armed with a cricket bat.

'Why the hell did you lock me out?'

'Forgot you weren't here. Sorry. I thought you were a burglar.'

'A burglar would no doubt have made a neater job of getting in.' Rod shut the door of the smelly room. 'I groaned when I saw I had to come in through that dreadful loo.'

Dick put the cricket bat away, and they started to climb the staircase.

'Had a good evening?'

'Yes. Yes, very good.' Rod lifted his hands melodramatically. 'I discovered God, and Claudia and I are going to become a world-famous singing partnership.'

'You're mad.'

'Goodnight, Dick. Sorry I woke you up.'

'I didn't hear Rod go.'

'We didn't know where you were. He passed on his thanks.'

'I was sorting, right upstairs. Endless sorting. I like Rod. Now, don't go to sleep on that sofa again, Claudia; it's quite ridiculous to spend half the night getting cramp when you could be in bed.'

'Yes, Ma.'

'Well, get up then.'

'Yes, Ma. In a minute. Just a minute.'

'When I come back from the kitchen I want to see that sofa empty.'

'It's such a comfy old sofa. Why can't we take it over to the new house?'

'It's far too big and you know it.'

To admit the truth, I don't want to move either. I'm dreading being all cooped up. Well, I'll be away soon, end of the year, whoopee, freedom here I come. What a blissful thought. Except there's Gerry. But he'll be here when I come back in the vacations—Claudia, how I've missed you, Yorkshire was such a dull place without you. Oh yeah? I can see him missing me, I can just see him. He probably wouldn't notice I'd gone until I came back: good God, it's Claudia, you must come and have lunch when I'm free . . .

What I must not forget, never forget, is that Gerry doesn't like singing, isn't interested in my voice or anyone else's. He'll never encourage me, never help me realize the dream. My Dream. At times like this it seems a folly of my imagination, no more. Me a singer—I can't even get it together in a simple folk

50

song. It wasn't Jo's fault she couldn't accompany me, and she knew it. I'm mean to Jo. I'm mean to Rod. Perhaps I shouldn't have asked him to play for me. He's good, though—I'm sure it will work out well. I just wish I hadn't asked him. I'm afraid— oh, never mind.

'Claudia . . .'

'Yes, Ma. Look, I'm going.'

5

God, looking very like Henry Dalton, angrily put a hand on his shoulder and shook him; then He disappeared leaving cold air behind but the hand shook him, shook him . . . chilly and unprotected, Rod began to reach for arguments . . .

Then he woke up. Kevin stood at the end of the bed, having pulled his blankets off.

'What's going on?'

'Ten o'clock.'

'Shit.'

Kevin left the room, and Rod turned onto his back. He tried to remember what his time-table was for the day. A paper chase. He had to organize a paper chase. He shut his eyes; he felt exhausted. His brain and body were devoid of any will to exist. The memory of his euphoria the evening before left him unmoved. He could not even bring himself to reach for his blankets. He lay curled up, quite still.

'Rod! Rod?' Dick put his head round the door. 'Didn't Kevin wake you?'

Rod groaned.

'Come on, man. We need you. Now.'

It was a joyless, apathetic day. The boys were uncooperative, Claudia was uncommunicative, Nora irritable. Everything Rod did, said or heard was flat and tedious. He tried to redeem the day by asking Claudia when they could meet and rehearse their songs.

'Some time. I don't know.' She continued scraping carrots.

'We'll need plenty of rehearsal—'

'Don't fuss.'

'I warn you, Claudia, I'm not doing it unless we rehearse the thing fully—'

'Don't fuss, Rod. We'll rehearse till it comes out of our ears. But not today.' She heaved the heavy saucepan full of carrots onto the cooker.

'Thanks for last night, by the way.'

'Oh. Yes.'

'I really enjoyed it. I liked your family—'

'More than I do sometimes.' Claudia disappeared into the larder and started an acrimonious argument with Nora who was in there sorting leftovers.

'Is it you, madam, who puts the veg all jumbled together—I like the potato separate—'

'Oh, what the hell, Nora—'

Rod retreated, and went up to his room to lie on his unmade bed. His habitual, chronic untidiness made the room look as though a catastrophe had occurred; every conceivable surface was thickly littered, the drawers of the small chest hung open, clothes spilling out; the bedside table bore a tottering tower of books, each marked with old envelopes, strips of newspaper, empty paper bags. When Rod finished a book he usually forgot to retrieve his marker. The only thing he ever put away was his guitar into its case (now under his bed, on top of his shoes).

He picked up a thriller, but having opened it let it flop onto his face. Claudia possessed his whole mind; he tried to push her image out by thinking of his family about whom he felt guilty—he must write them a letter, he really must. But Claudia returned laughing, peevish, singing, serious. Nice, nasty. Her changeability excited him almost as much as her physical presence. And he realized that whenever their relationship took a step forward (as it seemed to have last night), she made sure it was followed by a step backwards.

Maddening, contrary Claudia. Damn you.

He must have slept, because a tap on the door disturbed him. Nora came in.

'You've missed supper.'

'I wasn't hungry, thanks.'

'Are you feeling ill?'

'No. Just one of those off-days.'

'My, what a mess.' Nora picked her way to the open window, where she lit herself a cigarette. 'Did you enjoy yourself at the Daltons?'

'Very much.'

'They're real dears.'

'You know the family, then?'

'Like my own kin. I met Di and Henry twelve, maybe thirteen years ago in Birmingham.' Nora gazed out at the dark garden. 'I've been close ever since.'

Rod sat up. 'I'd no idea.'

'That's why I work here in the summer. Henry arranged it.' She paused, her face full of memories. 'When I first had Jimmy, I lived with them for a few months. I don't know what I'd have done without them; gone mad.' She tapped her ash out of the window. 'I'm not even a Christian either. Never could get along with the church part of it.'

'So you've known Claudia since she was a child?'

'I have.'

'How strange.'

'Little baggage. That's why when I warn you about lady Claudia, I know what I'm talking about. She can hurt you.'

'Claudia's not interested in me.'

'But you like her.'

Rod was disappointed Nora didn't contradict him. 'I'm hopeless with girls anyway. I'm just a callow, inexperienced youth. Repeat callow, repeat inexperienced.'

'She's not the first girl you've fancied, is she? Pardon my asking.'

'Well in a way she is.'

'Then you can't help feeling inexperienced, can you? Got to start somewhere. Just wish for your sake it wasn't Claudia.'

'But Nora, she's fantastic—'

54

'There must be other girls you like back in London.'

'Not really. I was at a boys' comprehensive and what with work, sport and my old motorbike, there wasn't time for girls. Not that I was particularly interested—I suppose I'm a late developer.'

'I'm all for late developers. You've got the rest of your life to chase after sex.' Nora ground out her fag on the wall outside the window and threw the dead butt into the night. 'Though it's an over-rated pastime if you ask me.' She moved towards the door. 'Glad you're not ill, anyway.'

'Don't go. Tell me more about Claudia.'

She paused, her fingers on the handle. 'Dear Rod, you only want to talk about Claudia. And I only want to talk about lonely old me. Which is boring for both of us.' She went, leaving his room smelling of cigarette smoke.

Behind the pile of bedside books, propped against the light, was an unopened letter from Rod's father. Without conscious premeditation, he now tore it open and began reading. It was an entirely ordinary letter, except for the last paragraph.

'What I'm going to say now might not apply to you, but a conversation I've just had with Julia makes me nervous in case it does. Julia has been very up and down recently and she finally told me the reason: she apparently was sure she had been the main cause of my doing what I did last June. She was very upset. I told her, and I meant it, that this was nonsense. No one can be blamed for what I did, *no one*; except myself. So, in case like your sister you felt you might have been to blame—you weren't. That's a promise.'

Rod re-read his father's vigorous upright script, with its sharp edges, and sensed the emotional cost of this letter. He then folded the letter up and lay staring at the ceiling. His father had always been good at saying one thing and meaning another . . . what was written could mask so much.

Rod sat up, and said aloud: 'But why shouldn't I believe he

means what he says?' He put the letter aside, full of trust in it. He went downstairs and ate a huge number of biscuits washed down with a pint of milk. He then decided to have a bath. Baths at King's Thornton were not undertaken lightly; the water was often cold because the boiler malfunctioned—a fact the boys appreciated. Rod tried a tap: amazingly, hot water burst forth. There was no plug in the bath, however, and he tried two more bathrooms before he found one. As he sank into the water, he made a vow to write a long letter to his family tomorrow. He also decided to pay less attention to Claudia both in person and in his own mind. Friendly detachment was needed.

Claudia came up to him after lunch next day, smiling. She was dressed in a white shirt, red skirt, and bright scarf round her neck. No eccentric touches today. She held out a piece of paper.

'There's the list of songs. The final choice depends on you.'

'Let's have a look. I know at least half these—and I could learn the rest. No problem.'

'Some I sing much better than others. For instance, I like *Don't think twice it's all right*, but I don't always do it well.'

'That's one I don't know.'

'It's good. It's a man's song but I don't think that matters.'

'You're sticking to folk.'

'That's what they asked for. But we could slip in a jazzy blues number.'

'Great. When shall we practise?' All day and all night would not be too much.

'I'd rather not do it here. Come down to the house on my day off.'

'Fine.' The two days he had to wait stretched for ever. 'Fine.' But life was warm and bright; everything was possible. It might even be possible Claudia liked him. When she was in a good mood, no one was so golden. He forgot all about friendly detachment. It also slipped his mind to write to his family.

Wednesday came at last. Rod made sure he was free in the

afternoon, and hurried down to the village. Claudia had said
'come after lunch'. The church clock said half past one, and he
decided it was too early yet. He wandered across the square
into the post office-cum-stationer, where he had noticed a few
books for sale. He browsed through the meagre selection, and
his eye was caught by a title on a black spine: Rolle: *The Fire of
Love*. He drew it out. The cover consisted of a serene medieval
picture showing angels and men adoring the Lamb of God
against a background of woods, hills and spires. A dove in a
nimbus hovered above the Lamb.

'You can have that half price.'

The copy was indeed very battered. The large woman behind
the counter nodded encouragingly at Rod. Half-willingly, he
went over to pay for it.

'The vicar'll be pleased. He insists we have one of those Rolle
books for sale.' (Rod noticed she pronounced Rolle to rhyme
with 'dollar'; Dalton rhymed it with 'hole'.) 'This one's been
here ages, as you can see. I'll tell him I let you have it half price.
He supplies the copies we sell; it's daft really—' She talked on,
and Rod held his book to his chest and edged his way to the
door. Another customer arrived, and he escaped.

Quarter to two. He must wait until two. He sat down on a
bench in the middle of the square and opened the book at the
very beginning and read Rolle's first two sentences.

*I cannot tell you how surprised I was the first time I felt my
heart begin to warm. It was real warmth, too, not imaginary,
and it felt as if it were actually on fire*—Rod, finding this
description akin to his feelings about Claudia, looked eagerly
through the rest of the book. He saw with dismay how 'religious' it was, how fixed on defining the solitary life of the
mystic. There was nothing here for him. He nearly took the
book back, half price or not, but knew he couldn't now;
Thornton was too small a place for his action not to be reported back to Dalton. The clock struck two and he jumped
up, tucking the book away into an inner pocket.

Men were working on the new vicarage; one was painting

57

the front door, another was up on the roof. A lorry was delivering gravel; Dalton was directing it. He waved when he saw Rod. Then Di Dalton appeared from behind the old vicarage and smiled in surprise when she saw him.

'Hullo there. What can we do for you?'

'Claudia asked me to come and rehearse the cabaret.'

'Ah, yes. Did she. She's out at the moment. What time did you fix?'

'Now, after lunch.'

'I'm sure she hasn't forgotten.' Di Dalton did not look sure. 'She went to Ripon this morning: I expect she'll come back on the two fifteen bus. Excuse me a moment while I take this rake to Henry.'

Rod stood awkwardly waiting, unable to accept Claudia's absence. He looked back up the road, but it was empty.

'Come and have a cup of coffee with me.' Di led the way round the side of the house. On the paved York-stone area outside the kitchen there were deckchairs, and a tray with the remains of a snack lunch for two on it. 'Sit in the sun while I get it ready.'

Rod pretended to read a newspaper, wondering whether he should go or stay. Claudia had forgotten all about him; he was sure now. Di came out with mugs of coffee, chatting to him about the move. Rod sat half-listening, tense in Claudia's unexplained absence.

'She would have been here by now if she'd caught that bus, wouldn't she?'

'What? Oh, yes, I suppose she would. She is naughty, forgetting about you. I'm afraid she's an unreliable girl in that way. It makes me despair sometimes.'

'I think I'd better go.'

'Oh, dear. What can we do? I expect you've kept the whole afternoon free for her.'

'I had rather.'

'Stay if you like. It's not much fun, but you could help Henry spread gravel. He'd be extremely grateful for another pair of hands. Then when Claudia turns up, you'll be here.'

So Rod stayed and helped Henry, relieved that they were working too busily for conversation. He kept an eye on the gate. When the job was done, Henry took him over the new house. It echoed as they walked round and smelt strongly of new plaster and concrete. The whole house looked raw, naked; the windows were placed curiously high in the walls, giving each room a prim, blind air. Rod looked out of one at the old house. He had never been particularly aware of the shape of buildings, but the contrast between this mean place and the generous bulk of the old building across the garden struck him forcibly. And there was Claudia walking up to the big front door. Claudia.

His pleasure and anger at seeing her were equal. As he watched, Di Dalton intercepted her and an argument ensued. Claudia cut this short by hurrying over to the new house, her expression difficult to read. Rod waved from his window, but she did not see him.

'Rod?' Her voice reverberated round the empty house. 'Where are you?' Her footsteps thundered up the narrow stairs. 'I really am sorry. I missed the bus, I hadn't forgotten you.'

'That's all right.' Anything was all right, anything: he felt warm and forgiving, faced with her obvious remorse.

'It's not. We've missed a practice. And I see you've been used as unpaid labour.'

'I've enjoyed it.'

'Ma and Dad are dreadful. They're always dragooning people into helping—'

'Claudia, what nonsense, we don't *dragoon* anyone—'

'You make it impossible to say no, then.'

'Well, I enjoyed it.' Rod nearly added that it helped to pass a painfully empty afternoon. 'There's still time for a short rehearsal.'

'Right.'

They went over to the main house and found Claudia's

handwritten bundle of songs, copied out from various collections in the Folk Club.

'Most folk songs are about either freedom or love, I've noticed. I decided to stick to songs about love for the cabaret—some are very well known, one or two are not familiar at all.' She shuffled through them. 'I thought we could kick off with *The Oak and the Ash*, since it's a North country song and more general than the others.' She read out:

No doubt, did I please, I could marry with ease;
Where maidens are fair, many lovers will come;
But he whom I wed must be North country bred,
And carry me back to my North country home.

And it's got a chorus for everyone to sing, so that'll break the ice at once. I thought we might have another rousing chorus song at the very end, something corny like *Careless Love*. Have a look through these—how many do you know?'

Rod flipped through the pages covered with her large scrawly writing. 'I don't know *Wildwood Flowers* or *Don't think twice it's all right.*'

'They're both good.'

'Sing me the tunes.'

Claudia started to hum *Wildwood Flower*, but Rod stopped her. 'With the words. I need the words so that I can mark the chords.'

I will dance, I will sing and my laugh shall be gay,
I will charm every heart, in his crown I will sway;
When I woke from my dreaming my idols were clay
All portions of love had all flown away.

They worked on the haunting tune until Rod had made a note of the main guitar chords needed. 'Right. I can now work that up into a decent accompaniment.' He looked at his watch and groaned. 'I've got to go.'

'Do you want to play a solo in the middle?'

'Heaven forbid. Claudia, I really must split. I'm late already. Dick'll kill me.'

'I'm sorry about the bus.'

Rod packed up his guitar hurriedly, trying not to wonder whether she had in fact missed the bus or whether she had just forgotten him. As he was leaving, Henry Dalton called down the stairs.

'Wait a minute, Rod. I've got something for you—payment for all your efforts this afternoon.' He handed Rod a book wrapped in a paper bag.

'Thanks—but there's no need—'

Dalton tucked it into the folder of music Rod was holding. 'Hope you find it interesting.'

As he walked up the road out of the village, Rod peeped into the paper bag. There he saw another, identical, copy of Rolle's *Fire of Love*. He started to laugh. It was too ridiculous. He hardly wanted one copy, let alone two.

When he got back to King's Thornton he looked for a suitable bookcase into which he could slip the extra copy. The general bookcase in the common room held a battered collection of comics, thrillers and boys' stories. He hesitated to put the Rolle amongst them. Nora came in on some errand.

'A present for you, Nora. By a strange coincidence I've got two of these.'

Nora gave a quick glance at the books and smiled. 'I can see you've been to the Daltons. Henry's always doling those out. Why did he give you two?'

'He didn't. I bought one first. So have the spare.'

'No use giving it to me, love; I never read—got no time. Give it back to Henry.'

'I don't want to offend him.'

'You won't offend him, silly boy. Henry's not like that. He'll just be pleased you bought your own.'

'I hadn't thought of that.'

'Dick's been looking for you.'

'I'm late, I know. I'll do extra duty tomorrow.'

He ran up to his room and threw the two books on his bed. They lay neatly side by side; the mythical countrysides seemed to join: there were two Lambs, two groups of adoring angels, two nimbuses; a dual revelation of glory. Disturbed for a moment, he put his guitar on top of them. Truth was truth, after all; repetition made it no truer.

'ROD! Come down here, you rotten son of a nameless Cockney she-cat—'

'Keep your hair on, Dick. I'm coming.'

'I should hope you blinking are.'

I am perverse. There's no doubt about it, I am perverse. *That Rod is the best thing that's happened to me as far as my singing is concerned: he believes in my voice, he really likes it, and what's more he plays well himself. We're a good team with great potential. It's exciting. And what do I do, but avoid him and put off rehearsals and generally behave as if I didn't care about singing with him. I can't stop myself. I am hopeless, I really am. Tomorrow, tomorrow we'll have a fantastic rehearsal together: we'll go up on the moor and really beat it out.*

'Claudia, is that you?'

'Yes, Ma.'

'You're late.'

'It's been an exhausting day. The bad weather's driving the boys wild; they keep erupting.'

'Have you eaten yet?'

'Couldn't face mince and treacle pud. I just want a salad, some cheese; nothing much.'

'I'll get it for you.'

'Thanks. Where's everyone?'

'Henry's got a meeting. Jo and Evie are over at the hall playing badminton. By the way, Gerry just rang.'

'Gerry.' *Keep your voice cool, dear Claudia, but cool. Blast, blast, blast, I could have come home earlier too—oh despair, despair.*

'He said he'd ring back sometime.'

I've heard that one before. He never rings back; one try is all he ever manages. 'Or I could ring him. Did he say what it was all about?'

'*Some exhibition or other he thought might interest you.*'

She's got a funny look on her face, Ma has, as if she suspects something. She's too canny.

'*Boring.*'

'*Then don't bother to go.*'

'*I probably won't.*' *Casual yawn. But underneath I seethe, wondering what Gerry was really after: an exhibition is possible, but it could also be a convincing smokescreen. As soon as I can I'll ring him back. I must control my unseemly haste . . .*

'*What about some fruit salad?*'

'*No, thanks, Ma. I've had plenty. I'm not really hungry.*'

'*Well, eat enough. The telephone can wait.*'

'*Who said I was going to telephone?*'

6

Rod did not like Claudia's new song, *Don't think twice it's all right*. It told the story of a man leaving his love because she had failed him unwittingly; given him too little, taken too much.

'You don't sing it as well as you sing the others.'

'I need practice, that's all. I've never done this one in public.'

'It sounds wrong coming from a girl.'

'Oh, don't be so rigid. Why should that matter? The sentiment is universal.'

'I was just saying what I thought.'

'But it's a good tune, isn't it?'

'Nothing wrong with the tune. I like it, in fact.'

'Well, don't listen to the words.

'It ain't no use in calling out my name, gal,
Like you never did before.
It ain't no use in calling out my name, gal,
I can't hear you any more.
I'm a-thinking and a-wandering all the way down the road
I once loved a woman, a child, I'm told
I gave her my heart but she wanted my soul.
Don't think twice it's all right.'

The guitar sounded thin out in the expanse of the moor, but Claudia's voice seemed stronger and clearer than ever. She tried out the new song several times. Then she stopped.

'Perhaps you're right. Maybe I shouldn't do it.'

'I was just changing my mind and thinking you ought to. Try

the last verse again. I've got a new idea for the accompaniment.'

As they practised, they saw Kevin starting from the house up the path in their direction. Rod frowned.

'What's he coming up here for? You didn't ask him to, Claudia, did you?' She laughed at him. 'I wouldn't put it past you—our rehearsals always get interrupted.'

'I think we've made progress today. We're much more of a team. We know each other's style better.' She leant over and kissed his cheek. 'Thanks for agreeing to do the cabaret.'

By the time Rod had put his guitar down she had moved out of reach. 'I'm doing it because I like being with you. That's the only reason—' But Claudia was watching the path below.

'Here's Kevin. Hi. That was quick. You don't hang about, do you. A minute ago you were down at the bottom.'

Kevin looked thoroughly put out when he saw Rod, the guitar, and sheets of songs spread on the turf. Rod glared at him, Kevin glared back.

'Rod and I were rehearsing.' Claudia started to collect up the music. 'You must come and hear us perform.'

'Where?'

'At the local Antiquarian Society do in a couple of weeks. We are the illustrious cabaret.'

'I don't dance.'

'How odd, I'd have thought you would. Perfect physical co-ordination and all that.'

'I'm going up to the lead mine. Come?'

'Oh. Yes, all right. We'd more or less finished, hadn't we Rod.' Claudia put a stone on the sheets of paper. 'Come too.' She looked insistent.

'I don't feel in the least energetic.' He tried to sound light-hearted, offhand. 'I think I'll lie here and kip. Wake me if you pass back this way.'

'Fine. See you later then.' She turned, and followed the rapidly disappearing figure of Kevin. 'Hey, wait for me, you horrible fit freak.'

Rod lay back with his eyes shut, cursing Kevin yet again, cursing Claudia, even cursing himself for not going with them. He could feel the touch of her lips on his cheek still, as definite as an itch. He rolled over on the turf, knocking his guitar so that it twanged. He had never kissed a girl properly in his life. He had never wanted to kiss any of the girls he knew, Julia's friends, even though there were two he quite liked and had taken out occasionally. He wanted to kiss Claudia. And hold her; his thoughts went into a turmoil at the thought of her body. He had sisters who never locked bathroom doors and sometimes wandered about naked; the female body was no mystery to him. Yet whenever he saw either of his sisters nude, their breasts and pubic hair were always a slight shock, beautiful and strange. The firm curves and small nipples with their surprising circle of browny-pink flesh, the thick neat patch of hair at the base of a white stomach were female, adult, little to do with the Julia who was making a fig-leaf with her hands in mock modesty, or the Lucy who was in a faraway dream as she cleaned her teeth. Rod knew they felt the same from the way their glances rested with covert uneasy interest on his genitals whenever—rarely now—they saw him naked.

He lay face downwards for some time, watching the ants and various other insects that passed close to his nose. Oh to be an ant, to escape from this infatuation, obsession; this love. The fire of love. Life was wonderful when he was with Claudia; at almost every other moment it was difficult to endure. He leapt to his feet and, collecting up music and guitar, hurried down to King's Thornton. If she did return that way, he wasn't going to be there.

He had another hour or so before he was on duty again, so he picked up the spare copy of Richard Rolle and headed for the vicarage. He rang the bell twice and was about to leave when a workman shouted: 'He's there somewhere. Ring harder.'

Henry appeared at last, dusty and dishevelled. 'Hullo, Rod. Come in. Claudia's not here, though—'

'I haven't come to see her. I brought this back; you see, I've got it already and it seemed stupid not to tell you.'

'Of course. Let me give you a replacement—'

'No, you don't need to—'

'Please—I would like to. Follow me to the chaos of my study, which I'm sorting out.'

The large room was full of books; many were in stacks on the floor or crammed into cardboard boxes. There were files and cabinets along one wall, overflowing with paper.

'Now, what can I give you—' Dalton prodded a row of paperbacks. 'Unfortunately for you, most of my books are of a religious bent. Here, what about this: *Science versus God*—basic stuff, a friend of mine wrote it, but not bad at all. You're a scientist, aren't you?'

'At the moment.'

'Well, you might have some fun with it.'

So Rod, expressing genuine thanks but feeling faintly got at, put the book into his pocket. Yet he liked Henry Dalton; there was an immensely sympathetic quality in his gaunt figure and lively eyes. Henry stepped backwards and a pile of books fell over in a dusty cascade.

'Oh, damn.' He sighed. 'Moving the contents of this room is a wholly daunting prospect.' He and Rod bent together and piled the fallen books up again. 'How's the cabaret getting on?'

'Not bad. We need a lot more rehearsal. Claudia tends to be elusive.'

'Claudia is the archetypal holder of the theory that every-thing-will-be-all-right-on-the-night. She continually avoids near-fiasco because she possesses talent and quick wits, but one of these days they are going to let her down. She needs disci-pline. Make her practise, Rod.'

Make her practise? I can't *make* your maddening, beautiful daughter do anything. I love her, I hate her, she consumes me, but she's elusive and I'm so inept that we'll never ever do more than—'I'll try to, sir.'

'Don't call me sir, for heaven's sake. Henry. Henry.' He lifted a pile of folders and files tied round with string. 'These

68

contain all my copious researches on Rolle. Every time I start to work on the book itself, the sight of these weighs me down. I suffer from scholastic timidity; I check and double check and clear, heartfelt writing goes out of the window.' Henry gazed at Rod, then swung the pile towards him. 'Rod. Take these down the garden and set fire to them. Go on. I'll never write the book unless they are destroyed.'

'I couldn't.'

'Yes, you could, it's just a heap of paper.'

'I honestly couldn't. Ask Claudia to do it.'

'She'd dance around the pyre chanting spells. I ought to do it myself. Perhaps I will one day.' He dropped the files into a large cardboard box. 'One day.'

Someone began to play a plaintive tune downstairs on the piano. Rod wandered over to the fireplace, above which was a reproduction of Michelangelo's Adam being brought to life by God's hand. 'Since I came up to Yorkshire I've started thinking again about various problems I thought I'd solved to my own satisfaction.' Rod spoke slowly. 'I find I haven't solved them at all.'

'Such as?'

'Well, the existence of God for example.'

Henry laughed. 'Would that we could "solve" that one. Proof positive is what man wants, and he will never get it.'

'How can you be a priest without it?'

'I sometimes wonder. I have my faith, my belief; but to those who need proof, it doesn't seem much. Mind you, it is worth examining very closely what is meant by "proof".'

Rod drifted to the window. After a long pause, he said: 'Out on the moor the other night I came as near as I ever have to believing in God.'

Dalton sat down on his desk, tired, dusty, and suddenly withdrawn. 'Don't trust experiences on moors. The hills themselves are so splendid they induce feelings of reverence which in my experience have little to do with belief.'

'It wasn't a feeling I'd had before, so I wouldn't know.'

'I am rebuked. Tell me what you used to think.'

'If I bothered to think about him at all, I came to the conclusion he didn't exist.'

'There's an old story about Napoleon, who asked an astronomer where the action of God came into his calculations. "Sire", was the reply, "we have no need of that hypothesis".'

'In a way, that's what I still think. Except that astronomy in particular raises ultimate questions which no one can answer, and then I begin to wonder.' There was another pause. The pianist began to pound out Tchaikovsky. 'I must go, or I'll be late. Dick will get annoyed with me again.'

'I've enjoyed our talk.'

'So have I. Thanks for the book.'

'And you get my recalcitrant daughter to rehearse that cabaret. Pin her down. Tell her I shall be angry if the thing's a fiasco.'

'I'll work on her.'

Work on her—kiss her, that's what I want to do. And I bloody well will. A little action from me is what the situation needs . . . As Rod ran back to King's Thornton, he imagined a series of situations in which he could kiss Claudia. He was put out when he saw her bicycling towards him on a curved and deserted part of the long drive up to the house. This was not one of the situations he'd imagined.

She stopped and got off her bike. 'Hey, what happened to you? Kev and I doubled back on purpose to pick you up, but you'd gone.'

Rod did not answer. He was panting and sweaty from running. He looked fixedly at Claudia's left earlobe; hair hung down in untidy tendrils from the loose knot on her head. He suddenly stepped forward, grabbed her shoulders, and aimed a kiss at her mouth. She neither pulled away nor responded, but instead rang her bicycle bell. This startled him, and she laughed.

'Rod, Rod, fancy you behaving like a churchyard rapist.'

'Damn you, Claudia.'

70

'Don't rush off. I'm only teasing.'

'You're always teasing.'

'Maybe I am, but you should relax a bit more. You're always so tense.'

'Only with you.'

She turned her head aside, gazing up the drive as if she heard something. Rod found the appealing lines of her head, neck and ears under her untidily gathered hair almost unbearable.

'Oh despair, despair,' he said.

'What's the matter now?'

'Never mind.'

'Look, I'm just going down to the village to fetch something for Nora. Let's rehearse again later. What about after supper?'

'We certainly need to rehearse as much as possible.'

'I'll come up to your room, if you like.'

'Yes. No. I mean, my room is a complete shambles.'

'Or we could use Nora's sitting room if she doesn't object—'

'No, let's use my room. It'll be more private.'

But there was no opportunity for rehearsal later because two of the boys were missing and as darkness deepened a search was mounted. Friends said that Sean and David had gone out on the moor during the afternoon and not been seen since. Kevin and Claudia knew the moors best, so Dick paired Rod with the former and himself with Claudia and they set off. Kevin and Rod, plus an old-fashioned loudhailer, were given the moors above the house to search; Claudia and Dick took the moors across the dale, where there was a popular walk to a ruined cottage.

'Neither of those two boys seemed the adventurous type,' said Rod after twenty minutes' silence as they paused above a small waterfall. Sheep, disturbed by their passing, cried on the slopes round them.

Kevin lifted the hailer. 'Sean! David! Are you there?'

His voice was surprisingly loud. Sheep scattered in panic. Rod and Kevin flashed their torches around and listened intently. After a long silence, broken only by baas, they climbed to another eminence and repeated the process.

Rod, irritated by Kevin's total lack of conversation, said: 'If the boys had come up here in the afternoon, wouldn't you and Claudia have seen them on your walk?' When Kevin did not reply, he repeated his question; he would force him to talk.

'No. Moor's a big place.' Kevin did not look at him, but at least he had finally answered. Again there was a pause. Then Rod said, 'What do you think of our Claudia?' He was still angry with her and needed to hurt his image of her; yet the question seemed a betrayal, and he wished the words had not been said. Kevin replied immediately.

'None of your business.'

'Don't be so touchy. I just noticed you spend quite a lot of time in her company, that's all.'

Kevin stopped and turned. His eyes were fierce.

'Why shouldn't I?'

Because she's mine. I'm the one who loves her—'No reason why you shouldn't.'

'You think you can come up here with your London ways and take control—'

'I don't—'

'Arrogant sod—'

'You're far more arrogant, going round in total silence as if the rest of the world just isn't worth talking to—'

Kevin hit him hard, knocking him over. Rod jumped up and struck him back, sending the loudhailer flying. Kevin was in perfect physical condition and it was clear after a few minutes' vicious struggle that he would win any contest of strength. Rod pulled away suddenly, sickened at what he was doing. He shook his head, panting heavily.

'This is mad. To hell with it.' He picked up the hailer and rushed up the moor. He was shaking and bruised, and furious with himself for provoking the fight. Fool, stupid jealous fool.

'David! Sean!' he bawled through the hailer. He saw Kevin's torch-light disappearing down another valley. It was soon lost

72

to sight. Rod searched in vain until after ten o'clock, the time arranged for a rendezvous back at the house. His jealous fury soon abated into empty exhaustion, and by the time he entered the kitchen and saw Kevin there with all the others, he felt no emotion at all.

The boys had been found by Dick and Claudia. Darkness had caught them while they were out on the opposite moors. They were discovered sheltering in the ruined cottage, frightened of going any further through the ghostly shadows of the hills and valleys.

'We thought you were lost too, when you didn't return on time.' Claudia slipped to Rod's side, handing him a mug of cocoa.

'No great loss.'

'Come off it, Rod.'

'I went further than I planned.'

'You look shattered.'

Rod drank his cocoa, and leant back against the kitchen wall. Normally this murmured conversation with Claudia would have pleased him, but tonight all his feelings were dead. She stared at him with faintly puzzled eyes, and when she started for home a few minutes later, returned to his side to touch his arm and say goodnight.

Rod likes me too much, and now I've upset him. Why did he have to try and kiss me. It's no good, I can't love two people at once, I just can't. I haven't done anything to encourage Rod; I wish he'd accept he is my good friend and not want more. And he is my good friend; I feel as if I'd known him for years.

Ouch, that was a bat. I don't like bicycling through these wooded corners much even in daylight. At night it's all too creepy. Another bat. Faster, faster. Damn those boys for getting themselves in a jam.

Rod looked dreadful when he came back, and he had a bruise on his face. Kevin looked steamy too—perhaps they had had a fight. They always look as if they hate each other. Anyone could hate Kevin, but no one could hate Rod. He's so amazingly nice, even when he's angry. There is a part of me, a tiny part of me, that's sorry I love Gerry and would rather I loved Rod.

7

The next morning everyone came down late to breakfast. Nora looked pale and distraught because of a letter she had received; she knocked a bowl containing twenty beaten eggs off the kitchen table, thereby depriving half the boys of their cooked breakfast because there were no more eggs until the farmer delivered a fresh batch at midday. Rod was one of the last to come down; he shambled over to the hatch, stretching, relieved to find his emotions back to normal as he looked in the kitchen in vain for Claudia. Not knowing about the recent culinary disaster, he teased Nora about the scrappy food and was appalled when tears came into her eyes. She moved quickly away. He went round into the kitchen.

'Nora? What's **up?**'

'Nowt.'

The kitchen floor was an eggy sea, on which Nora had flung sheets of newspaper. 'Disastersville. Claudia'll be here soon, she'll help you.'

'It's Claudia's day off.'

'Oh. Yes. I always forget.' Wednesdays came round quicker than the other days of the week. He had already been in Yorkshire three weeks. He gazed blankly past Nora. Three weeks.

'It's just one of those bad days.'

'Let me give you a hand, Nora, before I take the boys down to Thornton.'

'No, love. I made the mess.' She blew her nose on a handkerchief so large it looked like part of a sheet. 'But there's something else you could do for me.'

'Ask away.'

'Would you drop in on the Daltons and tell Henry I need him? I've—I've got a problem; had a letter today that's a bit of a shock; he's the only one who knows all the ins and outs. Any time today, tell him. Just come when he can.'

'I won't have much opportunity—I've got twenty boys to look after.'

'Do try, Rod, there's a friend. I can't get away at all on Wednesdays.'

'Why don't you ring up?'

'Hate the phone. Always say the wrong thing.' She sighed. 'Oh well. If you can't make it you can't make it. I'll ring him.'

'Leave it with me.'

Rod had planned to take his boys to see Thornton church. Although none of them had been inside, there was a chorus of groans when he suggested it.

'Aw no.'

'Only if we can all go to the shop after.'

'Right. Church first, then shop, then a walk down the valley.'

'What are the other lot doing with Dick?'

'I've no idea. You're stuck with me, and that's the itinerary. Has everybody got their picnics? Off we go then.'

Claudia was standing in the triangular market place, waiting for the bus. She was leaning against a wall, rather ostentatiously reading a paperback of Jung's *Modern Man in Search of a Soul*. She was dressed in a wild mixture of colours, orange, purple, bright blue and green; she had bare feet, and her sandals were dangling from her belt. She bowed in Rod's direction, put her hand in exaggerated horror over her eyes at the sight of the twenty boys.

'Hi. Is your father around?'

'He was earlier.'

'Where are you going?'

She hesitated. 'Ripon, if you must know.' She lifted her book back into reading position. Rod felt his day had got off to a bad start. He chased after the boys who were aiming for the village

76

shop.

'Hey. You go there afterwards.' He collected them together as the bus arrived. They watched Claudia get on it.

'Why isn't she up at the house?'

'It's her day off.'

'She sings good, Rod, doesn't she?'

'Sings well. Yes, she does, when she puts her mind to it.' He could hear himself sounding like a schoolteacher. It was so easy to cut oneself off from children by talking stiffly. 'Go on, Keith, what did you like about the way she sang?'

'I dunno. It was good, that's all.' Keith dropped back.

Rod led his group into the churchyard, pointing out the slit gate which allowed human legs to pass but not the fat bodies of sheep. The boys swung through it, shouting and whistling.

'Watch out, Tom, you fat slob, you'll get stuck.'

They ran off over the tombstones, vaulting the smaller ones. Rod eventually rounded them up in the church porch. As they went noisily in ahead of him, despite his useless plea for quiet, he began to regret having brought them. To his relief no one else was in the church; the chatter and laughter from the boys seemed overwhelming.

'*Ssshh*. Please be quiet, you little monsters.' He tried to interest them in the misericords, the old clarinet, the tattered standards hanging above. Hardly any of them paid attention; they milled about, banging up and down the wooden pews. One of them found the little staircase up into the belfry and was on his way up it until Rod got him by the ear.

'It says No Entry.'

'Never saw the notice.'

Two boys were giggling right up by the altar; they appeared to be touching the altar cloth. Rod felt fear and anger, and shouted: 'Right. Outside, all of you. Fast.'

As the last boy left, Rod turned and stared round the church to make sure it was empty. The boys had left a psychic smear behind; the air seemed imprinted with their restlessness and careless disturbance. Rod still shook slightly with anger; he

77

could hear them shouting outside, and wished he could stay where he was and abandon them to amuse themselves.

The sound of Henry Dalton's stern voice made him hurry out through the swing doors which creaked and huffed as they shut behind him. Henry was wearing his black cassock which made him look taller than usual. His expression softened when he saw Rod.

'I couldn't think what was going on.'

'I brought the boys here as part of an outing—'

'Fine, good. I hope they found the church interesting.' Most of the boys had already slunk through the gate, and Henry grinned at Rod. 'Or did they?'

'Not their scene. They didn't do any damage though.'

'Why should they?'

Rod hesitated. He had no doubt that minor destruction had been imminent when he had made them all leave. 'Nora sent a message.'

'Oh?'

'Could you possibly go up and see her today sometime? She says she's got problems.'

'Ah.' Dalton gazed vaguely up at the great trees at the edge of the churchyard. 'Haven't we all? Have you come to find Claudia?'

'No, no, I'm in charge of those boys all day. Besides, I saw her get on the Ripon bus.'

'Oh, did she? I was under the delusion that she was going to stay at home today. That was the plan at breakfast.' He turned and smiled a little sadly at Rod. 'As you have no doubt already discovered, our Claudia is a mercurial lass.'

There was a series of shouts from the village square. 'I must go and see what the little devils are up to.'

Henry walked with him to the gate, picking up sweet papers dropped by the boys. Rod hurried away and found the boys clustered round the stone cross in the middle of the square. On top of the cross was a ginger cat; Sean was busy trying to climb after it.

'Down! Come on, Sean. I would have thought your exploits yesterday were achievement enough for this week—' Rod led them into the shop. With the exception of this short period of shopping, the boys clearly found Rod's outing a bore. As he walked back to King's Thornton in the afternoon, with the trail of tired chattering boys behind, he realized how in their eyes he was already on the other side of the fence: an adult, a teacher. He turned round; the two nearest boys immediately lowered their conversation. He was no longer of their kingdom.

'You don't usually do breakfast on your own. Where's Nora?'

'It was time she had a full day off. I came up here early so that she could catch a train. Dad drove her to the station.' Claudia gave Rod an egg, boiled solid; he peeled it and mashed it up with margarine. When he had finished his breakfast he offered Claudia help because he was free for an hour.

'Wash up if you like.'

'Is Nora O.K?'

'A bit desperate, I think. She gets like that periodically. My parents defuse her and life goes on as before.'

'She asked your father to come here and see her yesterday.'

'Oh. She's always doing that. Whenever she has a crisis she immediately contacts him and pours out her troubles.' Claudia stacked plates and mugs beside Rod. 'I once thought, influenced by the endless romantic fiction I read at fourteen, that Dad was Jimmy's father. I had this vision—not of Nora and Dad as great romantic lovers, ha ha—but of Nora loving Dad and begging him to give her a child so that she could taste the joys of motherhood before it was Too Late. Dad, in the spirit of Christian love and sacrifice, of course did so.' Claudia laughed as she crashed down a saucepan full of dirty cutlery. 'One thing wrong with that theory is Jimmy himself: he doesn't look the least bit like Dad, and not like Nora either. Which postulates Another Man.'

'It's hard to see Nora in the role of heroine and deserted lover.'

79

'She's basically attractive, you know. Good figure, good hair, nice eyes. She could look fantastic if she took any interest, but she doesn't give a damn. I love Nora.'

Rod piled clean mugs in a towering apex on the draining board. 'What's good about Ripon?'

'Why do you ask?'

'I thought I might take a look at it. Is it worth a visit?'

'See Ripon and die. It's just a small market town with a minster and a lovely market place. And a good baker of meat pies. It's worth a visit, I suppose.' Claudia undid the belt of her jeans and tucked the vast man's shirt she was wearing in more efficiently. She was barefoot as usual; her feet were grubby, but she had painted her toenails carefully and these gleamed as she padded round the kitchen. 'Did you realize the dance was two days after we move? And we move a week today.'

'Chaos.'

'You're telling me.'

'We must rehearse. We must rehearse.'

'I've decided to sing a blues instead of the folk song you don't like. I can't decide which—'

'But I've been working on the accompaniment for that song. It's been a sweat composing it.'

'Oh. I hadn't thought of that. Then we'll keep it in, if you're happy about it. I might do a blues as well.'

'About that song, a mad idea occurred to me.'

'Yeah?'

'That we should sing it together. A duet. It might give an ironical flavour—could be effective.'

It was hard to read Claudia's reaction. Rod at once lost confidence in his idea.

'Forget it.'

'No, why? It might work. I didn't know you liked singing.'

'With you, all is possible.'

'Come off it.' Claudia stowed the last of the milk jugs in the fridge. 'When that's finished, get your guitar and we'll practise now. Just for half an hour. Come on. Hurry.'

80

When the last plate had clattered into the rack, Rod flew upstairs to fetch his guitar. He bumped into Nora's Jimmy on a landing, and as he apologized took a quick look at his face. Indeed, there was not the slightest sign of Henry about him. Claudia was full of mad fancies.

They rehearsed very successfully; the tall old kitchen had a resonant acoustic, and both were in the mood.

'Doesn't the guitar sound good in here, Rod? We'll be doing the cabaret in a marquee—with lousy acoustics I should think.'

'Microphone?'

'I'll refuse to use it. If my voice isn't big enough, too bad.'

'It is.'

'Now, let's do *Mary Hamilton*. I always think I know that one, and in fact there are parts where I'm shaky.

Word is to the kitchen gone
And word is to the hall . . .'

she sang; they caught each other's eye and smiled at the aptness of the words. Then Rod had to bend his head over his guitar to hide a sudden access of joy: never had he and Claudia been so at one. And she sang so beautifully: the clear notes, with a hint of depth and darkness in them, poured from her throat with natural ease. Rod was aware, from his own limited singing experience, how difficult it is to begin the first note of a phrase cleanly and truly. Claudia had no problems: her notes broke each silence with limpid perfection. *Mary Hamilton* lay just right for her voice, and she flung back her head at the most poignant moments and sang with great feeling.

'If you do it like that at the cabaret you'll have them all in tears.'

'I doubt if the crowd at this dance could be moved to tears by a song. I warn you, Rod, they'll be a square lot, with a few shining exceptions. Expect the worse. We'll just do our thing and enjoy it, and too bad if it's not to their liking.'

'Our programme should appeal to them, it's not exactly way out—'

'Folk was what they ordered.'

'There's nothing wrong with the songs. They're just not very original—'

'Except for our duet. Come on, the time has come to try it out. Choose a key that suits both our voices. How low is yours?'

'I'm sort of tenor. High baritone, to be precise.'

As they sang lines like:

'And it ain't no use turning on your light, babe,
I'm on the dark side of the road.
Still I wish there was something you would do or say
To try and make me change my mind and stay,'

the fact they were singing in unison gave an ironic twist to the words that was right. Claudia stood behind Rod, who sat on a stool to play; she seemed to echo his voice, and they decided this added a dramatic touch. Rod had a powerful but hoarse voice which blended curiously well with Claudia's. Some lines he almost spoke against her full, well-pitched tones.

'That's brilliant.' Claudia danced round the kitchen. 'It's exciting. In fact, we really are becoming good together. We're an act, we're an act.' She swept her long loose hair off her face with her hands, then picked up a rubber band and made a pony tail. 'Too hot to wear it loose.'

'You must have your voice trained, Claudia. Seriously. It's too good to waste.'

'Maybe.'

'No maybes. Your voice is good enough to make singing your career.'

'Ah, Rod.' Claudia stood looking out of the kitchen window; she clenched her hands in front of her face. 'If you only knew. If—well, I'll tell you. I'll tell you my most secret dream. I want more than anything, more than *anything*, to be a singer. But it sounds so crazy—how can I, an ordinary girl with no money and no musical connections, get anywhere, even begin?'

'With your voice nothing's crazy—I keep telling you, it's a rare voice, a gift from the gods. I'm sure of it.'

'But how can you be so sure? What do you *really* know

about singing?'

'Not much, I agree. It's just my gut reaction. I'm sure you've got whatever it takes. Haven't other people told you?'

'Other people—they know even less than you. The teacher who takes singing at school doesn't like me and never gives me a chance. And our church choir is all male, very conservative. No solos there either. So there's been no one qualified to judge my voice; to tell me if it was good. What I must do *now* is find a teacher.'

'Haven't you tried?'

'Of course I've tried; there's no one round here. For years I've been scheming and dreaming about my voice. Yet I felt there was no hurry, because I read somewhere that a woman's voice doesn't really start developing until late in her teens. I feel now the moment is right. So what I must find is someone who'll take me back to square one, and teach me the ABC of technique so that one day I can sing anything, knowing precisely what I'm doing. At the moment I sing well by accident.'

'Happy accident.'

'But happy accidents aren't good enough. I must be able to sing all the heart and gut songs from folk to grand opera in such a way that it still sounds natural, accidental, but in fact have a rock-solid technique.'

Rod stared at Claudia in some awe; she filled the kettle and plonked it on to boil. 'It'll be a hard life, Claudia.'

'I don't give a damn about the hardness of life: if it's hard it's hard and that's it. I refuse to play for safety.'

Rod struck a dramatic chord on his guitar and Claudia laughed.

'So how are you going to start your career as a great singer?'

'Get into Cambridge if I can.'

'Why Cambridge?'

'It's supposed to be the best place for music. Not that I'm going to read Music, I couldn't at the moment, I hardly know a tonic from a dominant, but I've been told that all singers and performers go to Cambridge if they can—they get so many good opportunities there to perform. I'm going by the student's Alternative Prospectus, and they ought to know.'

Rod watched her put coffee powder into mugs; he wished with all his heart he had considered Cambridge when he was deciding which university to go to, instead of ruling it out. Too late now. He swallowed, and turned away, propping his guitar on the window sill. Claudia went on talking.

'Anyway, it seems sense to get a degree in something in case my voice doesn't develop or respond to proper teaching, and all my dreams come to nothing. Sugar?'

'Come and stay with me in London, and we'll go to the opera.'

'Listen Rod, you mustn't say a thing to anyone about all this. No one else knows.' She blew on her coffee, eyeing him uneasily. 'I wish I hadn't told you. I have a superstitious fear that if you tell people things that have been secretly important, it's dangerous. Not only because they might let it out . . .'

'Why then?'

Claudia paused. 'It gives them power over you, knowing what they do. And also, sharing a secret sort of diminishes it.'

'You can trust me.'

'It isn't a matter of trust.'

'I won't tell a soul—'

'Oh, I know that. Yes, I trust you there.'

'Well, then.'

She shrugged, finished her coffee, and put a cardboard box full of potatoes onto the draining board. 'I shouldn't have told you.'

'Don't worry.' He touched her arm, aware of new currents of feeling between them. She shook him off. 'Why do you always have to push me away?'

'Oh Rod, because. Because.' She tipped a flood of earthy potatoes out; they tumbled into the steel sink. 'Take no notice of me.'

'That's impossible. I can't help wanting to touch you—'

Claudia turned on the tap so fiercely that water ricocheted

off the potatoes in a spray all over her. 'Whoops.' Her wet shirt stuck to her flesh and Rod could see her nipples clearly through the soaked cotton. She grabbed a teacloth and started drying herself roughly. 'I really must get on with the work, or no one will get any food.'

Rod picked up his guitar, and went reluctantly to the door. Claudia remembered something.

'By the way, do you drive?'

'Yes, I do.'

'Brilliant. Because we'll need a car to get us to the cabaret—the dance takes place about ten miles away in a fairly isolated house. Dad's going very early so we don't want to go with him—but I think I can borrow a car from an old parishioner who lets Ma borrow her Mini any time—I'm sure she won't mind—'

'Look, Claudia, nobody's going to lend a car to be driven by an unknown teenager—'

'Well, Miss Topham won't know precisely who's driving if she's not told.' Claudia giggled. 'Are you a good driver?'

'Yes. Actually I am. But you're completely unprincipled—'

'Don't be stuffy—'

Claudia's breasts were still partly visible, and Rod decided he could not stand their proximity any longer. 'You fix it up. I'll be chauffeur. See you.' He went upstairs and stood in the middle of his room, his eyes shut and his whole body tense.

Now what was that opera I saw the other night on the box—Traviata, *that's right, La Traviata, by Bellini or somebody. No, Verdi, of course; I am so ignorant—despair, despair. Anyway, the heroine, Violetta: that singer was fantastic, she really was. She was such a good actress, and so passionate and natural. I watched her very closely, and I noticed that when she sang she held her face in a certain way as if all the muscles inside her head and throat were somehow open and relaxed. And her breath control—some of the lines she sang went on and on with no strain at all. It made me feel very third-rate. I wish I could remember her name.*

I keep thinking about her technique whenever I'm singing. I wish I could do things she could do. The announcer said she had studied for years before her début, much longer than is usual these days, because she wanted to have an absolutely sound technique. Even that word technique makes me shiver with excitement. I must find a teacher soon, I must. After the cabaret, I'll really start asking people to help me. That is, if the cabaret goes well. I feel it's a test.

What was it that soprano said, the announcer repeated it twice: 'Many people have beautiful voices but few know how to sing.' Here's one of them, lady. Even my lovely encouraging Rod would agree with that.

8

'Rod? Ah, there you are.' Dick came bustling into his room, clipboard in one hand and pencil poised. 'I've been doing a bit of planning—we always try to make the last week something special.'

Rod stowed his guitar under the bed, waved Dick to a crowded chair and then sat down on rumpled blankets. He forced himself to empty his mind of Claudia and listen to Dick's plans.

'Working backwards, I thought on the final Friday we could have a barbecue followed by a treasure hunt in the dark and end with a sing-song round the old camp-fire. Then on Thursday perhaps you could organize an entertainment of some sort—the staff could do a silly play for the boys perhaps—'

'Thursday's bad—that's the day the Daltons move.'

'Doesn't concern us, does it?'

'It affects Claudia—she'll take that day off I'm sure. Besides, I've promised to help for a while too.'

'Ah. Yes. I see the problem. Well, I'll give Kevin that evening to organize the barbecue and your do can be on Friday. It makes no difference.' He chatted on, full of ideas and suggestions. Nothing daunted him; every situation was full of possibilities. Rod, for whom any current situation that did not include Claudia held no interest, gazed at him blankly.

'Come on, Rod. A little enthusiasm from you would help.'

'Sorry. Yes, I'll cook up a play or something. When do the boys go home?'

'Saturday morning. And you?'

'I hadn't thought. There's this cabaret on Saturday night—'

'What cabaret?'

'You've surely heard that Claudia and I are providing the cabaret at a local dance.'

'No.'

'You must come, Dick. We'll need moral support.'

'I was supposed to be going back to Sheffield on Saturday—'

'Stay on. We'll all go to the dance. Perhaps Nora would come too.' Rod was animated again; Dick was infected by it.

'Well, I could. What sort of do is it?'

'A dance given by some local organization in a country house. I'm sure we could smuggle you in as our road manager. Nora could be our dresser.'

Dick giggled. 'What a gas. I haven't got any clothes here except jeans and that—'

'Nor have I. They'll have to lump it.'

'People tend to be formal up here at dances, you know. It'll be a lounge suit affair, by the sound of it.'

'Too bad.' Rod stretched and went to the window. Distant shouts came from the games pitch where Kevin was playing cricket with the boys. 'What's the programme for today, by the way?'

'A coach is arriving at one o'clock, and we're all going to Ripon and then Fountains Abbey.'

'The boys will love that—they so appreciated Thornton church.'

'Yeah, I heard. But Fountains is all ruins, lots of space for belting about. Those who aren't interested can amuse themselves—take a football or something.'

'Let's hope they don't use it to ruin the ruins.'

Dick got up and went to the door. 'I'm going to ask Claudia if she'd like to come—there's room on the coach.'

'You do that.'

Claudia came, because everyone agreed to have fish fingers and baked beans for supper. (Nora disapproved of convenience foods and stocks were therefore high.) The coachload sang noisy songs all the way to Ripon, where they were set down in the large market place at the heart of the town.

'Right. The three groups will stick to their leaders,' shouted Dick. 'No boys disappearing off in ones and twos. We all meet here at the obelisk at two forty-five sharp. Everyone take a time check.'

All round the remains of the morning's market were being cleared. Attractive houses flanked the square; in the distance was the Minster. Rod's group of boys spent some time wandering round the few stalls still in operation, until he managed to persuade them that a walk round the town was a good idea. Claudia had gone off on her own. He had suggested she could be his guide, but she had laughed and said Ripon was too small to get lost in. Rod found Ripon and its Minster disappointing, but he knew it was mainly because Claudia had not stayed with him. With ten minutes to go he urged his group along a steep, twisting street leading back to the market place.

'Can we go into that shop, Rod?'

'No.'

'It's got really good model cars—'

'No time. Keep going.'

But at that moment Rod saw Claudia come out of a side door just off the street. A lorry thundered past obscuring her, and when it was gone he saw that a dark-haired man was standing beside Claudia, his arm round her shoulders. Rod could only see the man's back view; Claudia's face was visible. Rod dodged into a shop doorway, but could not stop looking. Claudia was talking; she seemed to be pleading with the man; he pinched her cheek while he answered, making her smile. Then he bent to kiss her goodbye. Claudia clung to him, her arms round his neck. Rod turned away, pressing his face against the shop window, his feelings overwhelming him. His group of boys had all disappeared into the toy shop, but he didn't care. All he could see were Claudia's clinging hands. When he turned round again the man had gone and Claudia herself was almost out of sight up the street.

Weak with jealousy, sick at heart, Rod stood gazing at a

window full of women's clothes, unseeing. One of his boys came out of the next door shop and shook his arm.

'Look at the time—it's ten to.'

'Oh. Yes. Get the others, Simon. Quick.'

The coach was loaded and the engine ticking over when they reached it. Dick looked angry.

'You're late. We've got a tight schedule—'

'Sorry.' Rod felt a burst of irritation at Dick's fussy voice. He stood for a moment at the front of the coach, delaying the moment of encounter with Claudia. At first it seemed she wasn't on the coach at all, then she leant out from a seat near the back and called him. He ignored her and started to talk to the driver. But the driver, a taciturn man at the best of times, said: 'Sit down, lad. No passengers standing.' Rod was forced to move down the gangway. The first empty seat was beside Claudia. She patted it. He wanted to ignore her again, but pride was pushed out. He sat down, his mind a painful whirl.

'Did you like Ripon?'

'Not much.'

'It's an interesting place historically—'

'The company of a dozen lively barbarians doesn't encourage one to seek out history.'

'True.'

'Was your time in Ripon fruitful?' Rod's effort to sound casual was a miserable failure.

'Fairly.'

The coach swung out of Ripon on the Fountains road. 'Actually, I went to see an old friend to persuade him to come to the dance so that he could see our cabaret.'

'I think I saw you with him.'

Claudia flashed Rod a quick look. 'Yes. You might have. Gerry is an old family friend, one of Dad's great admirers. I'd like him to hear our act because he has lots of contacts—he's the sort of person who knows everyone.'

Her clinging hands . . . her expression as she talked to the man . . . Rod had them clearly in his mind's eye. Yet Claudia talked about this Gerry so offhandedly, as if he was indeed just an old family friend. Rod could only believe her. He felt the frozen pain in his heart melting. He had exaggerated everything, read more into the situation than existed; he was a jealous fool, as usual. He had a sudden desire to laugh maniacally, to shout his relief. A bag of toffees was passed under his nose at that moment, and eating them kept both Claudia and himself silent for a while.

Claudia stayed at his side during the mile-long walk through the wooded valley of the river Skell with its landscaped pools, vivid lawns and carefully chosen trees and shrubberies.

'Isn't it beautiful? The perfect sort of park. I love Fountains, love it.' Claudia walked with a serene, relaxed expression. 'It's one of the special places.' Ahead of them, on a bridge over one of the little waterfalls, waited Kevin and Dick. The boys had all gone ahead. The four walked amicably together, united by the exceptional beauty of their surroundings. When the Abbey came into view, its pinkish-buff stone was glowing in the afternoon sun; the ruins seemed to float above the bright green grass around.

'It's so big,' said Rod in amazement.

'Largest ruins in England.' Dick was looking at his guide book. 'Begun 1134.' He read out further disjointed chunks in a monotone.

Rod was unprepared for the beauty of Fountains. He liked old churches, and he liked ruins, but the emotional see-saws he had experienced that day had pushed further anticipation from his mind. The splendour of the Cistercian Abbey wholly awed him; he gazed at the columns, the variety of arches, the elegant vaulting, the carved stone round the soaring, empty windows, and could not speak in answer to the comments of the other three. In the Chapel of the Nine Altars, the remarkably tall, thin, fluted columns, supporting corbels and arches of delicate beauty, moved him in the way some music did. He gazed at those columns until his head swam. Beside him Dick's voice read: 'one of the noblest examples of Early English . . .'

His voice droned on, breaking the spell.

Then Rod saw Claudia waving at him from a far doorway, and escaped towards her, leaving Dick and Kevin to their guide book.

'Come and look at the cellarium. It's stupendous.' She took his hand and led him through the cloister. He held fast to her hand, dazed by all he was seeing and feeling. At the far end of the intricately vaulted cellarium, three hundred feet away, there was a group of strangers, but otherwise the place was empty. Its extent stunned Rod.

'How did all those monks do it.'

'God knows.'

'I don't think I can take any more in.'

'I know how you feel.'

Rod shut his eyes, and put his arms round Claudia. They stood for a while together, until a group of their own boys came in and started wolf-whistling. Claudia laughed, but Rod left the building impatiently. Dick was outside gathering everyone together. It took him so long that in the end he had to use a whistle to summon the last stragglers. Tired and footsore, they began the trudge back to the car park. Rod, on his own at the tail of the group, turned to look at the ruins before they disappeared from sight. The stone was even pinker in the dropping sun. He felt he had left a part of himself at Fountains, as if the elevation of stone had drawn some quality from his soul as a payment of praise.

There must be other buildings in the world where spirit and matter are so united, but I don't know them yet. There can't be that many—

'Rod! Rod!'

'Coming.'

Claudia did not wait. As Rod turned to follow, a park-keeper went by with a spiked stick.

'You with those boys?'

'Afraid so.'

The old man felt in his pocket and brought out one of those

92

snow scenes enclosed in a dome of liquid. It was small and crude and had a squirly label across its base declaring it to be 'A present from Yorkshire'.

'One of them dropped this. They didn't hear me shout, and I can't run after boys any more.' He handed it to Rod and walked on.

Rod shook it idly as he hurried after his party. Flakes whirled round a rough replica of Ripon Minster. Ripon. Claudia's hands round the neck of that man . . . He had the intuition, which he quickly suppressed, that her explanation about the man was not the whole truth.

When he got back to the coach again he was the last. Claudia was sitting next to Kevin and since she was on the outside, she must have joined him. Rod held the paperweight up as he passed down the coach.

'Whose is this?'

But it belonged to no one.

'Would anyone like it?'

The boys, out of shyness or disinterest, did not answer. With a flourish, Rod presented it to Claudia. 'Madam, a valuable memento of a place close to your heart.'

Claudia bowed as she took the ugly object.

'Ah, thank you, kind sir. How touching.'

Her face was flushed. A while later Rod saw her lean across Kevin and throw the paperweight through the open window. It smashed against a wall.

Sometimes I'd like to break the world as I broke that stupid paperweight. Why did he give it to me . . . he's devious, we're all devious. We all go round scoring off each other, meaning one thing, saying another.

And Gerry. If only Gerry—the hell with it. I wish I hadn't gone to Fountains. Fountains is still His Place; every time I go there, he's in every arch, through every doorway. I'll never forget the way he made me see it as it had been, whole, full of monks; and I'm sure it isn't just because he trained as an architect; it's Gerry himself who makes everything so heightened, so special. Oh, I wish I didn't love him, why do I still love him. I'm sure he doesn't love me any more . . . if he ever did. He did, he did once, perhaps he still does.

I shouldn't have smashed that paperweight. I just couldn't help it. It was so ugly. Rod looks very fed up. If Gerry hadn't been in my life already, I'd have . . . oh, despair. I like Rod's eyes so much. He's not afraid to show his feelings. He's . . . he's authentic. I'm a mean cow.

'Toffee?'

'No thanks, Kevin, not at the moment.'

'Your exam results come yet?'

'Don't. I have heart attacks whenever I see a postman.'

'What subjects?'

'English, French, History. Grades, grades, grades. I'll never get to Cambridge.'

'Why Cambridge?'

'That's my secret.'

Gerry really doesn't believe in my voice. I can't get him to see

I'm serious. I wish he'd come and hear the cabaret—I know I'm singing better than I ever have before. Rod gives me confidence. He really cares. We must rehearse again today, later. I've got to the point with some of the songs when they just happen by themselves. I can feel my voice, my heart and my head are all together and what comes out is exactly what I want. Sometimes I'm sure it's just a question of getting the breathing perfect—oh, for a good teacher. I long to work and work and work at my voice—I know I make mistakes doing it on my own. £278, no, more, £281 I think—if Dad knew I'd saved that much up he'd be staggered. And all for that future teacher . . . Perhaps I'll be another Callas. I sometimes feel powerful enough . . . Gerry doesn't believe in my voice. I must get him out of my system.

'Nora! Why are you back so early?'

'Everything took less time than I expected.'

'We've all been to Fountains. Now we're going to have fish fingers and beans—don't disapprove—and you're not to do anything. It's still your day off. Go and have a drink peacefully on your own somewhere and I'll call you when the amazingly delicious meal is ready.'

'I don't want a drink on my own. I'll lay up the tables.'

'Oh, Nora. You're hopeless. You'd just wither away without work to do.'

'I would too.'

She could still look good if only she'd try—she's quite striking under the mess. Dad has always said she's a handsome woman . . . I'm never going to give up like that, never. Something's dead when you get so uninterested in your own appearance. I must get my black satin trousers cleaned for the cabaret. With the red shirt—no, it's torn—Mum's green silk would be best. I must look out something jazzy for Rod—

'Hi, I was just thinking about you—about clothes for the cabaret—'

'You're wanted on the phone.'

95

It's Gerry. I can tell by Rod's face. He's never rung me here before. Help. I feel sick.

'Hullo. Gerry?'

'What about a jaunt this evening? I've got to go to Richmond—something's cropped up since I saw you. We might grab a spaghetti there, and talk.'

'Oh fantastic, Gerry. I'll be finished here at eight. I'll whizz home first—'

'Don't bother. I'll collect you from King's Thornton. I've already told Di and Henry you're coming out with me.'

'Oh. Fine. What a lovely surprise.'

'See you at eight.'

Wonderful Gerry. I'd hate anyone else to boss me around, but he's different. I could fly. I was wrong. He does care after all. I could burst. Oh dear, I hope Rod isn't still in the kitchen. All clear. One more week of this slog and it's over; I've had enough kitchen work to last me a lifetime already. Oh, blast—

'Quick Nora, I've really cut myself on that lid.'

'Don't get blood in the baked beans.'

'Could add a little flavour—'

'It's a deep cut. Silly girl. Put it under the cold tap for a while before I bandage it.'

'Right thumb. I am a fool.'

'By the way—keep still—Rod said don't forget you've arranged a practice tonight.'

'Oh. Yes. What a nuisance.'

Why do we need another practice today? We had such a good one this morning. Fuss, fuss, fuss.

'Are you being cruel to Rod, my girl?'

'For heaven's sake Nora, why should I be?'

'Search me. You lead these poor boys such a dance.'

'I do not. Ouch.'

'You do. Blood's coming right through the plaster. You need a thick bandage. For some unaccountable reason they all flock after you, and as far as I can see you lead them all on. That's cruel. You can laugh.'

96

'Defamation of character. I know I'm foul, Nora, but I do not *lead them all on*. And I've been specially nice to Rod, with the result that he now won't leave me alone. I can't win.'

'This cut might need a stitch, you know. It's a bad one.'

'It'll be all right. Bind it tightly.'

'You go and eat now. I'll do the serving.'

'No, Nora, honestly this doesn't hurt. I'm not eating now anyway. Dad's friend Gerry Wells has got business in Richmond, and he's going to take me and give me a meal there.'

'I see. Rod seemed to think your rehearsal this evening was all fixed up. How are you going to get out of that one?'

'Nora, please stop nagging me. Everyone gets muddled and double-books. I'll explain to Rod—nicely.'

'This Gerry Wells, he's old enough to be your father—'

'He's not. Anyway, what's wrong with a family friend taking me out. Di and Henry know—'

'Nothing. Nothing at all.'

'You've got a suspicious mind, Nora.'

'Long training.'

Twenty to eight. I wish they'd all get a move on. Rod has hardly begun. He looks pissed off, but what can I do. And everyone's chatting and messing about just when I'm in a hurry. I'll go and clear the tables, that might speed them up.

'Claudia, what have you done to your hand?'

'Cut it.'

'Blood's coming through the bandage.'

'I know.'

And it's agony. Ten to eight. Blast. Gerry will just have to wait. I'll never get this lot cleaned up and put away before he comes, even with Dick and Kevin washing up.

'Give me that cloth. I expect you'd like to glam yourself up. Go on, Claudia, give it to me and scram.'

'Oh, Nora. You are an angel.'

'Which is more than you are.'

I wish I wasn't wearing this old shirt. Never mind, these

97

cords fit well. And Gerry likes my hair down, so that's easy. Tart my eyes up a bit. Wash my feet in the basin. No towel. No loo paper. This place is hopeless.

'Claudiyah! *Front door.*'

'*Coming . . . Hi, Gerry.*'

'*Amazing house. Can I just look round for a moment?*'

'*Go ahead, do.*' *Damn him, why don't we just go. I don't want everyone peering at us.* 'It's a shambles now—years of local education authority have left their mark.'

'*Good structure. I like the grand staircase.*'

Don't go up it. Please don't go up it. Rod is bound to come down. Someone is coming down—it's Kevin. At least he won't hang around and chat to us.

'*Claudia.*'

'*Kevin.*'

'*Do you know where the dartboard is?*'

'*No idea.*'

'*Where's Dick?*'

'*Outside, last I saw of him.*'

Gerry, please hurry. What's the point of nosing round this horrid place, with its smell of grubby boys and cabbage. Now he's gone into the television room. Groans.

'*Come on, Gerry. I need to get out of here.*'

'*Patience, dear Claudia. I've always wanted to see King's Thornton. That picture, presumably, shows it as it was in its palmy days.*'

'*It's a rotten painting.*'

'*Handsome place, once upon a time. Is that statue of Mercury still standing?*'

'*Statue? I've no idea. Never noticed it either way.*'

'*Unobservant child.*'

'*When I'm here, I'm working hard.*'

'*What have you done to your hand?*'

'*Cut it.*'

'*Well, if you're ready, let's go.*'

'*If I'm ready—*'

But I do love him, even if he always gets the better of me. And I like his old open car too, specially in summer.

'This is a lovely surprise outing, Gerry—'

'Look. Under the trees over there. Isn't that the statue of Mercury?'

'Could be.' *Oh, you're not going to stop again. Well, I'm bloody well staying put.*

'Come and look, lazybones.'

'Oh, all right.'

When I am with Gerry, I am lost. I am lost.

Gerry's been gone so long. I've been waiting hours in this car. Why didn't he take me in with him. My hand hurts and I'm hungry.

'Oh, there you are, at last.'

'Well, that was a very successful discussion. The gallery is just right for a small exhibition. I've booked it for my own show early December. Was I very long?'

'Ages.'

'Sorry about that. Never mind. Food and drink is what we need. And then a little talk.'

'Little talk—you make it sound ominous.' *Why should my heart lurch? Talk is one thing; a little talk usually means trouble.*

'What about this Italian place? I've heard good reports.'

'Any place will do. I'm starving. We had lunch early, before the expedition to Fountains.'

'How was it?'

'Lovely, but never so good as the day you took me there. You've spoilt it for me.' *Why did I admit that; it would have been better not to have told him.* 'I'm only joking, of course.'

'Now Claudia, what would you like to eat?'

'Advise me. I hate choosing.'

'What about some cannelloni to kick off with, and a veal escalope and salad?'

'Sounds perfect.'

99

Gerry never hesitates in restaurants. When Kevin took me out in Ripon, he was so nervous and undecided the waiter just went away and ignored him. Gerry gets a waiter's attention at once. I suppose he's an arrogant bastard really. I love arrogant bastards. But not when they want to have little talks ...

'How are Di and Henry coping with the move?'

'Not too badly, I suppose. Ma is depressed about leaving the old house. She does so love it.'

'They'll be better off in the new one.'

'I'm not sure.'

'It's compact, easy to run, easy to heat. Functional. The places we live in should be functional, so that our time and emotions are freed.'

'The old vicarage is very functional in its way.'

'Nonsense. It's beautiful, not functional.'

We are filling in time, talking about things that don't engage our feelings. I don't mind. I don't want the evening to turn sour.

'Well, the new house is not *beautiful*.'

'Eat up. Your food is getting cold.'

'This thumb of mine gets in the way.'

'What on earth did you do to it?'

'Cut it while I was opening a huge tin of beans. The cannelloni's delicious, by the way.'

'It is good, isn't it. Now Claudia, let's talk about you.'

'We've just been talking about me. I'd rather talk about you.'

'You.'

'There's nothing to talk about.'

'There is.'

'Come to my cabaret. I'll talk about that.'

'I told you I would come if I could. Don't nag me, dreadful child. Henry has offered me a ticket and I said I'd let him know definitely. Don't mention it again, or I won't.'

'Sorry.'

'What I wanted to talk to you about, my chicken, was this. I

*don't want to hurt you. But you must stop being in love with
me—it will do you no good. I'm the wrong person—'*

'*Gerry*—'

'*Please let me say what I have to. I'm the wrong person for
you—I'm too selfish, too old, and not very nice. If I'd been
nice, I'd never have encouraged you in the first place. It would
ruin my friendship with Di and Henry if they knew. I mind
about you, and I mind about them. I'd hate our family
friendship to be spoiled*—'

'*We can go on as we are—why change things*—'

'*No, we can't. You're too dependent on your feelings for me,
and it's not right. Today in Ripon you said something which
helped bring me to my senses.*'

'*What? What did I say*—' *Oh God, I can't bear this conversation, I don't want to listen. It's not really happening.*

'*You said you needed me to come and hear you sing because
my opinion mattered more than anyone else's.*'

'*It's true*—'

'*It shouldn't be, dear Claudia. And it isn't*—'

'*You don't understand.*'

'*My opinion is of no use to you at all. You only think it is
because, well, because you're infatuated. My opinion is not
only no use, it's also harmful. I don't know anything about
singing; I don't much like the way you do it; I don't much like
the songs you sing. I'm not musical or interested. You could be
very good at singing, and I wouldn't know. I could disparage
you, hurt you, put you off for life*—'

'*Let's forget about my voice, it's not important. I wish I
hadn't told you about the cabaret, I wish I hadn't dropped in
on you today*—'

'*I'm glad you did. Very glad you did. Seeing you running up
the street also brought me to my senses, I don't know why.
Perhaps because you suddenly looked so young*—'

'*Ouch.*'

'*But you* are *young. Eighteen is nothing.*'

'*Thanks very much.*'

'Claudia. Don't be hurt. But I must say it out plainly once and for all. You mustn't love me; I don't love you. I'm weak enough to have fooled myself into thinking I did. And therefore deceived us both.'

I thought those anemones were real but now I realize they're beautiful fakes. Red and white checked tablecloth. I want to put my head down on it and cry my heart out. I can't eat any more. I wish the world would stop.

'Those flowers aren't real, though they look as if they are.'

'What? Oh, yes. Claudia, look at me.'

'They're the best fake flowers I've ever seen.'

'Claudia. I feel dreadful about all this. Look, my love, let's finish eating and go and talk somewhere else.'

'But I'm not your love—'

'I shouldn't have started this conversation here.'

'I can't eat any more.'

'You've hardly touched your veal.'

'I'm sorry. I—I'll h-h-have to go and wait for you outside—'

Bloody, bloody man. I hate crying in front of people, I hate them to see, I hate crying, I hate men. I haven't got any tissues, I'll have to use my shirt. Bloody man. I want to die. Stop crying, Claudia. Stare at that castle keep, stare at its hardness until you stop crying. Stare. Hard, rough stones built by hard, rough men. Stare.

'Claudia. Come on, love.'

'Don't call me that.'

'Come on.'

'It's no good, Gerry. I can't stop loving you just because you tell me to.'

'You must try.'

'I'll always love you.'

'You won't. Love isn't like that. You don't believe me, I know, but you'll find someone else very soon, and wonder why on earth you were ever in love with that boring old Gerry.'

'I wish you were boring. It would make it easier. Go on— grow boring and fat and bald overnight.'

102

'That's my Claudia.'

'I feel desperate.'

'I'll tell you a little story which might help you. When I was seventeen I fell madly in love with a woman twice my age. Just about the gap there is between yourself and me. She didn't exactly encourage me, but she didn't repulse me either. The affair, if you could call it that, dragged on for ages. In the end I tore myself away—at that point I suppose I had begun to fall out of love anyway. She was obviously relieved. And I remember thinking to myself afterwards that she should have told me to push off long before, for my own sake. Selfish woman—I wasted months being miserable. So I'm trying to do just that; it hurts me to hurt you, but it will be better for you in the end.'

'I can't believe such misery is good for anyone.'

'Claudia. Look, a walk on the moor would be good for both of us. Yes?'

'Yes.'

'Cheer up. It's not the end of the world.'

But that's just what it is. The end of the world—my world with you. For you, it's a relief to shrug me off. I can see it is. Oh, it's unbearable. I ache, my thumb aches. I want to die.

'And you've got university ahead of you—every door is open, Claudia. Have you had your results yet?'

'No.'

'I'm sure they'll be good.'

'I'm not. I'm not sure about anything.'

'Claudia. Please. Don't start crying again. Please.'

'Sorry. It's been a long day. I'm whacked.'

'It's tough for you, that kitchen job. And exhaustion tends to heighten one's emotional reactions. I'm beginning to think a walk on the moor is not such a good idea after all. I'm going to take you straight home so that you can get a good night's sleep.'

Gerry, Gerry, please don't start behaving like a kind uncle. I think I could bear that least of all. I'm a woman, not a child.

'All right.'

Oh, despair, despair.

9

Rod saw Claudia drive away in an open car with the man she had been talking to in Ripon. He tried to force himself away from the window, but he had to be sure it was the same man. He saw the car stop, and the two of them (Claudia unwilling) get out to look at the statue. He stood frozen at the window long after they had driven off. 'Sorry, I've made a mistake about this evening—I had something on after all.' She had said it guiltily, but she had said it. She sailed through life taking what she pleased, making no efforts for anyone—

'Rod! Telephone!'

Nora's voice shouted from below. He went to the top of the staircase.

'Who is it?'

'Your father.'

Now guilt flowed through him; he hadn't written to his parents since the first few days; he hadn't answered their letters. He hurried down to take the call at the box in the front hall. People wandered about clattering, and it was difficult to hear or concentrate.

'Is that Rod Parrish? Rod?'

'Hullo, Dad.'

'How are you, stranger? We imagine that no news is good news.'

'I'm fine. I'm sorry I haven't written. Somehow letter-writing doesn't fit in with the busy routine here.'

Boys had scribbled all over the walls near the telephone; amongst the dense collection of signatures and graffiti, Rod saw 'Hurry up you bastard' and 'Fred's mum wears black

104

knickers'.

'Are you still there? The line isn't very good.'

'Yes. The phone's in a rather public position.'

'Well, tell us what you've been up to. Nell's on the extension.'

'Hullo, darling.'

'Hi, Mum.'

'Is the job interesting?'

'Very, thanks. It's good. I'm enjoying myself. Learning a lot.' Yet he sounded flat and unenthusiastic. He cleared his throat.

'Are the boys a bit much for you? You sound tired.'

'We've had a long day—we all went to Fountains Abbey.'

'Oh, Fountains, what a wonderful place—'

'Fantastic.'

'I've always thought it one of the most beautiful places in England. Such atmosphere. Not that I've been since I was a boy.'

Pause. 'How are Julia and Lucy?'

'Julia's gone off to her music camp. Lucy's here. I'll get her if you want.'

'No, don't bother. Just wondered if they were still alive.' Under 'Fred's mum wears black knickers' was a crude illustration of the garment.

'Did you get my letter?'

'And mine?'

'Yes, many thanks.' Two boys crashed fighting through the hall, making it impossible for him to talk. He waved them away. 'What did you say? I'm sorry about the commotion this end.'

'Have you met any nice people, made any new friends?'

New friends. The people at King's Thornton had become so much part of him, he could hardly think of them as 'new'. 'There's a nice crowd here.'

'Good. So you've had plenty to do in your free time, you've not been bored.'

'Not in the least.' Bored. Claudia, Claudia, tearing my life to

105

pieces. Perhaps boredom would have been better. Wonderful, dreadful Claudia. 'Quite the opposite.'

'Well, darling, this is expensive so we won't ramble on. When are you coming back? Sunday?'

'I'm not sure. I might be staying on a day or two. I'll let you know.'

'Mind you do. Nell will fret otherwise.'

'Oh, Alex, he can look after himself—'

Rod said goodbye and wandered into the kitchen, where Nora was reading a list and underlining various items.

'I see that wicked girl's deserted you.'

'Yeah. I don't mind, actually. I'm feeling flaked out.'

'Where does all the toilet paper go in this place? I keep ordering huge amounts, I put roll after roll out, and there's never any when you need it.'

'I'd noticed.'

'You'd understand if the place was full of girls, pinching it to clean off their make-up—but boys. There must be some explanation.'

'Diarrhoea.'

'You're talking to the cook, if you don't mind.'

'Is that Claudia's bike?'

'It is. That means she'll have to walk up here tomorrow. She'll be late.'

'I feel like a ride. I'm going to borrow it. She owes me a favour.'

'I thought you were flaked.'

'Riding through the night air is what I need.'

'Hark at him.'

'If I felt really noble I'd leave it down in Thornton for her.'

'Shouldn't bother, if I were you. Let her walk.' Nora pushed the clipboard away and tucked her biro in her pocket. 'I know I keep saying it, but don't let her break your heart. She's a tough cookie. I'd say you're not.'

'Tougher than you think, Nora.'

'You're a dear boy, that's what. She doesn't deserve you.'

106

'She hasn't got me.'

'Delighted to hear it.'

Yet as Rod bicycled away, he cried out to the trees: 'But she has, she has.'

Soft, yellowish light filled the dale; the low stone walls wriggling up the hillside were silvery-bright, the varied fields darkening patches between them. Hawthorn pushed flat by the prevailing wind grew close along the roadside wall like a mat of wiry hair. Its half-ripe berries were deceptively red in the evening light. Rod free-wheeled downhill, his heartache making him particularly receptive to each detail of the countryside. He disturbed a pheasant sitting in a tree by the road; it flew off with a feathery clatter, making him wobble. He took a turning away from Thornton, and bicycled for some miles until it was getting too dark to see well. The light on Claudia's bike was fitful and needed constant thumping. He aimed back for Thornton; just outside it there was a raised platform against a barn, where farmers left their milk churns for collection. Rod got off and sat on this for a while. He could hear cows lowing, and someone in the barn was washing out metal churns, singing loudly as they did so. Rod felt desolate.

'I thought it was you,' said Di Dalton.

Rod jumped down quickly. 'I was dreaming.'

'That looks like Claudia's bike.'

'It is. She left it up at King's Thornton. I took it for a ride before returning it.'

'Nice of you to bring it down.'

Together they walked into the village.

'If you're not in a hurry, stop for a coffee or a beer or something.'

'Thanks. I—yes, I will.'

Four large tea chests stood in the kitchen, filled with china, saucepans, stores. Everything was out of its place; the sense of confusion was total. Rod sat down on the kitchen table, noticing the usual assortment of briefs, bras and petticoats on the rack above him. Di poured him out a beer, and stared despondently at her kitchen.

'Let's move to the sitting room.'

Sipping the froth off his glass, Rod followed her.

'How's the cabaret progressing, Rod?'

'Not bad. We were supposed to be rehearsing this evening—' He stopped, annoyed he had said that.

'Oh, Claudia is a minx. She shouldn't have gone with Gerry in that case. That's too bad.'

'It doesn't matter.'

'Of course it matters. If she arranged to rehearse with you she should have stuck to that. There was no particular point in her going out with an old friend of ours anyway, she can do that any time. We see a lot of Gerry. No, I'm angry with Claudia. She's going through a stage when she doesn't seem to care whom she lets down or hurts. She goes too far.'

'Don't say anything to her.'

'I'm going to, Rod.'

'Please don't. She'll be so angry I came down here bleating to you—'

'But you didn't—'

'It would seem like that.'

'I suppose it would. Oh, I could put Claudia over my knee and beat her.'

There was a silence before Di went on: 'For your sake only, Rod, I won't. Does your sister behave with the same thoughtlessness?'

'I expect Julia would if she was as attractive as Claudia. I mean—guys don't flock after her . . .' He tailed off.

'It's hard to think of my eldest as a *femme fatale*.' Di gave a short laugh.

The clock struck ten, and Rod decided to leave soon in case Claudia returned. Then Henry came in and conversation continued.

Rod tried to leave, but found himself instead with more beer, deep in discussion. The front door banged and Claudia

108

stood in the doorway.

'You're back early,' said Di.

'My thumb's hurting and I've got a headache.'

'Is Gerry coming in?'

'No.'

'Pity. What's the matter with your thumb?'

'I cut it deeply on a tin.' Claudia did not look at Rod, and he kept his eyes from her.

'Let me have a look at it.'

'It'll be all right. It just throbs.' She was white-faced, and looked ill.

'Did Gerry get his business done?'

'Yes.' Claudia turned away and went to the foot of the stairs. 'It was a bit boring. I wish I hadn't gone.' She yawned. 'Goodnight, everyone.'

'I'll come up and look at that thumb. If I know you, it won't even be clean.'

'Nora dressed it.'

'I'll look at it anyway.'

Rod had risen and was hovering. 'I must go. Thanks for the beer.' He heard Claudia's footsteps upstairs; he bitterly regretted she had found him in the house.

'I'll see you out.' Di held the front door open.

'Please don't be angry with Claudia,' he blurted in an undertone.

'I promise I won't.' Di watched him run off into the darkness.

The next morning, a message came through that Claudia had gone to have an anti-tetanus injection and two stitches in her thumb and would therefore be late.

'I told the silly girl she'd need it stitched.' Nora was in good fettle; her day out had refreshed her. 'I told her not to come in but she insisted, though what use she's going to be one-handed I don't know. Her day off has been switched to tomorrow, anyway, for the move.'

'What else did she say?' asked Rod.

'"Oh, despair, despair," of course.'

During the course of the morning, Rod's A-level examination results were phoned through by his mother. Sick with apprehension, he learned that he had passed everything. Physics with the top grade, Mathematics and Chemistry a slightly lower grade, and History only just. He felt relief but no particular elation; he should have got good marks for Maths too; this had been expected of him. He wandered back to the kitchen, putting off the moment when he would have to take charge of the boys.

'Not good then? Didn't you pass?'

'What, Nora? Oh yes—everything. An A in Physics, otherwise a bit disappointing.'

Nora laughed. 'Dick, will you look at him. He's passed everything, and you'd think the opposite was true. Funny fellow.'

'I'm a perfectionist.'

'Claudia will probably have heard too.' Dick fished a half-smoked cigarette butt from the empty packet in his pocket. 'She was dead worried about them. Where is our ray of sunshine, by the way?'

'Gone to have her thumb stitched. No one mentioned any results had come.'

Claudia arrived just before lunch, wearing her yellow jersey and purple trousers, her hair in a severe knot and her eyes black with make-up. She called it her 'hangover get-up'. Her thumb was a ball of white bandage. For once she was wearing shoes, high-heeled sandals which clattered on the kitchen floor. They raised her eyes to a level with Rod's, and made her small bottom even more provocative. She went straight up to him.

'Congrats. Nora's just told me.'

'And you?'

She shrugged, her eyes sombre. 'Disaster.'

'Oh, Claudia.'

'English I just passed, French failed, and worst of all was

History, my main subject. I got such a low grade it won't impress any university, especially Cambridge. Not at all. I'll have to take them all again. What a prospect.'

Rod wanted to put his arms round her, but did not dare. Claudia fidgeted edgily.

'The awful part is, I thought I'd done well. The History questions were foul, but I really thought I'd dealt with them rather well. Perhaps the examiner didn't appreciate the special quality of my brilliance.' She cradled her bandaged thumb. 'Some brilliance.'

'You never know, the special quality of your brilliance could be just what gets you through Cambridge Entrance. They're not looking for run-of-the-mill intelligence, after all.'

'But they still won't like my grades. What the hell. I don't care what happens. I'm fed up with life.' She stalked off to the kitchen. She looked so unhappy Rod felt it couldn't all be because of her results. He wondered what had happened the night before. It was ignoble, unfair, but he felt a spasm of hope.

During the afternoon tea-break, Claudia sought him out again.

'Shall we have a little sing? It might cheer me up.'

'I'm free for an hour. Let's go up to my room; it's the only peaceful place.'

'Unless we go up on the moor.'

'I've only got an hour, no more.'

'Your room then. I'll just go and get my script.'

Rod left the door of his room open, and after what seemed like aeons of time Claudia at last appeared.

'Sorry I took so long. Nora waylaid me.' She glanced round the room, and made no reference to the utter confusion. She sat on the bed, took off her teetering red sandals, and curled her legs up under her. She leant back against the wall and briefly closed her eyes. 'I think it's the anti-tetanus jab that's making me feel so rotten.'

'Could be. How many stitches?'

'Three, I think. It feels like thirty.' She held up her bulbous

111

thumb. 'I'm going to disguise this unglamorous object at the cabaret by making a black satin sheath with black ribbons winding up my arm. I hope it'll look dramatic rather than odd. A white bandage would not exactly be good box-office.'

Rod tuned his guitar as she chatted on about the clothes he ought to wear. 'You fix it, Claudia. I'm not fussy. I'll wear anything you come up with.'

'Most men wouldn't trust me like that. I'm sure they'd be afraid of looking silly.'

'What order shall we sing the songs—have you decided?'

'More or less. We ought to finalize it now. Do you feel like introducing us, or shall I? I'd rather you did it, actually.'

'Oh. You know the people—oughtn't you to do it?'

Claudia laughed. 'After you. No, after you. I tell you what. Dad can do it. He's chairman of the society, so why shouldn't he? He makes fantastic speeches.'

'You know, I wouldn't dream of trusting my father to introduce me to a crowd: he'd be bound to say something squirm-making. He's one of those people who's overproud of their children's capabilities. But Henry's different, I admit. He'd probably be objective and witty.'

'He'll have everyone in stitches, and not at our expense either.'

'Right then. The Reverend Henry Dalton will introduce the brilliant double act of—what shall we call ourselves?'

'What's wrong with Rod and Claudia?'

'Claudia and Rod?'

'No, Rod and Claudia goes better. Come on, we're wasting time. Let's begin with our duet; it needs the most work.'

They forgot about the time, and Rod had to be fetched by Dick for his duty period. As they hurriedly packed up, they could hear Kevin barging about in his room next door. Before she left, Claudia went up close to Rod and said quietly: 'Thanks for cheering me up. You do it better than anyone.'

Rod stared at her. 'Even Gerry?'

'Gerry's a bastard.' She left. As Rod followed, Kevin

112

reappeared in the corridor. Rod stood back to let him pass with mock deference. Kevin hesitated.

'That girl means nothing but trouble,' he said brusquely. It was the longest sentence he had ever addressed to Rod. He then clattered off down the stairs. Between the two of them always hung the memory of their brief but vicious fight up on the moor.

> 'Kevin's taking us to the Zoo tomorrow, Zoo tomorrow,
>   Zoo tomorrow,
> Kevin's taking us to the Zoo tomorrow,
> We can stay all day.'

The boys sang at the top of their voices, stamping their feet at the word Zoo and quite drowning the sound of the guitar. The noise brought Dick and Nora into the common room, smiling and joining in the chorus. Rod sang the verses.

> 'Big black bear huff-huff a-puffin',
> Coat's too heavy, he's huff-huff a-puffin',
> Don't get too near the huff-huff a-puffin',
> Or you won't stay all day.'

As he sang, he noticed Kevin slip in; only Claudia did not come. Everyone in the room roared the chorus. The boys pointed at Kevin as they sang his name, and the song ended with earsplitting whistles and cheers. Kevin's face was bright red. He went up to Rod.

'Why my name?'

'It fitted best. Two syllables, lots of consonants.' Rod realized that Kevin was furious. 'Cool it, Kevin. You ought to be flattered.'

'Drop dead.'

Dick overheard this remark above the boys' chatter, and said loudly:

'Oh, come off it, Kevin. Don't be so touchy. Rod was only having a little fun—I can't see what you're so mad about.'

Kevin flashed a glance at the boys, who had now started to listen to what seemed like a promising row. Kevin opened his

113

mouth, shut it again and left the room slamming the door behind him.

'*Kevin's taking us to the Zoo tomorrow . . .*'

'Belt up, you lot. Out you go to play.'

When the room was empty of boys, Rod said to Dick: 'Kevin is weird.'

'I think he's jealous. He was definitely the boys' hero until you came along, and now he's not.'

'I don't believe you. I'm no hero.'

'You are to them. I've heard them talking.' Dick walked up and down, fidgeting.

'It's mad.'

Dick stopped and looked at Rod. 'Think yourself lucky. I've never been a hero to anyone.'

'Oh, Dick. You run this place so well—you're so full of good ideas, and so conscientious and caring. What does it matter if you're not a hero to the boys, whatever you mean by that? You're in fact the real hero in this place. You carry the can.'

Dick lit one of his half-cigarettes. 'I try too hard to get people to like me. That's my trouble. It always has been. It was the same at school. I was known as Suck-up Dick. I wish I didn't care about people liking me—Kevin doesn't care for instance—but I can't help it.'

'They do like you—we all like you, for God's sake. You're talking bilge.' Yet he knew precisely what Dick meant. No one liked Dick enough to seek him out and make a special friend of him, because Dick's eagerness was off-putting. 'Honestly, Dick, we all like you a lot.' Dick gave him a sad little smile, and left the room.

Rod took his guitar upstairs. He then made himself knock on Kevin's door. There was no reply, so he poked his head in. Kevin was lying on his bed.

'Piss off.'

'Don't get so sore at me, Kevin. I didn't mean to hurt you.'

'Everywhere I go there's you playing that bloody guitar and people singing. It's the lack of peace and quiet that I hate.'

114

Kevin's words poured out, as if he had been saying them over and over again in his head and now they overflowed.

'Sorry.'

'I come up here to my room to work and I'm driven mad by you and that Claudia.'

'Be fair, Kevin. If you'd asked us to stop we'd have gone somewhere else.' Rod kept his voice as calm as possible, feeling his dislike of Kevin welling up again.

'I hope you bloody enjoy her now you've got her.'

There was a silence as Rod stared at Kevin's pinched face. 'Sod you, Kevin. I haven't got her. She's got her own man, some guy in Ripon. She's not interested in any of us here.'

Kevin sat up. 'She is a bitch.'

'She isn't. She's just Claudia, and that's all there is to it.'

'She led us all on.'

'Did she? Speak for yourself.' He looked at Kevin's narrow bitter face, and could bear his company no longer. 'See you.' He hurried out of the room, out of the house, up onto the moor. He almost ran up to the customary lookout point, and then stopped dead.

Claudia was lying there face downwards. She leapt to her feet; her face was marked with weeping. She had let her hair loose, and it stuck out, full of pieces of moss and twig. She shut her eyes when she saw it was Rod who had disturbed her.

'What's the time?' she muttered.

'Nearly seven.'

'Oh, no.' She tore past him without meeting his eyes. He watched her bounce down the slope, her yellow and purple clothes luminous in the early evening light. Sheep bleated as she passed them; their distant grey bodies looked like short furry caterpillars as they darted distractedly out of her path.

Rod saw Claudia stop at a drinking trough fed by a stream. She bent over and splashed her face thoroughly with cold water. She then swung her legs over the estate gate and disappeared from sight.

'Claudia, Ma says please get up. The removal men are here.'

'They can carry me over, bed and all.'

All desire to move, to live, to do anything ever again has left me. And to crown it all we have to spend today squashing ourselves into that terrible jerry-built little box of a house . . . jerry-built. Oh God.

'Ma's getting mad at you.'

'Leave me alone.'

And I've got to re-take those hellish exams. Oh, I am a fool, a fool, a fool. I should have worked harder. It's such a waste of time, precious time. What am I going to do. Gerry doesn't love me. Did he ever—did he ever? Oh Gerry. I'd like to leave the country, disappear, go to Australia. Dear Manager, Sydney Opera House, I am a brilliant soprano as yet unrecognized here, but I am sure you would like to launch me on an astonished world . . . oh yeah. I feel so trapped, so trapped. How am I going to get through this next year . . .

'Claudia. Get up. This is ridiculous. The removal men are in the next room already.'

'Yes, Ma. Sorry.'

'What's the matter?'

'Nothing.'

'Oh, Claudia love, don't take it so hard.'

'I'm all right.'

'Come on, darling, we're all hating it as much as you are. It's painful leaving this dear house. I want to cry too. There, poor love, there.'

'I'll get up now. I'm O.K.'

116

'How's the thumb?'

'Middling.'

'Let me look. It's still a bit puffy. I hope it isn't infected.'

'I'll probably get gangrene.'

'What you must get is more sleep. You look really hollow-eyed.'

'Yes, Ma. I'll be down in a minute.'

But my hollow eyes, dear mother, are because my heart is broken. If you only knew the half of it. Thank God you don't.

10

'You're mad to burn them today.'

'Lift the other side of the packing case, would you. It's easier to carry with two.'

'Dad, I wish you'd listen.'

'I want them burnt. Today's as good as any. Do it for me, Claudia, please.'

Rod could see Henry's cheerful face; Claudia had her back turned. Tea chests and files lay all round them on the lawn.

'Ah, hullo, Rod. Nice of you to come.'

Claudia did not look at Rod; she bent and picked up an armload of files. 'Dad is determined on arson and I'm trying to stop him. But if you really want these burnt, so be it.' She marched off round the house. Henry asked Rod to help him with an overloaded packing case, and they followed her through to the corner of the churchyard where bonfires took place. Rod noticed the labels on the top layer of files: *Medieval Alliteration, Rolle's Calor, Dulcor and Canor, John de Dalton and other Patrons.*

'Who was John de Dalton, Henry?'

'Richard Rolle's first patron.'

'Any relation?'

'Another branch of our family. But the connection helped me to become interested in the first place.'

'*Calor* is heat, I guess. *Dulcor, canor* . . .'

'Sweetness and melody. I translate *calor* as warmth.'

They dumped the heavy case by the old bonfire. Clouds of flies rose, buzzed, redescended.

'There's a dead rat under that branch. Poof.' Claudia stood

back. Her father took a box of matches out of his pocket.

'You two will be doing me a great favour if you burn this lot thoroughly.'

'Dad, it seems mad to me to destroy all this work.'

'If I keep it, I'll never write my book.'

'If you burn it, you won't be able to.'

'Yes, I will. I've kept all the essential facts. All this is extra stuff, most of it done in order to put off writing the actual book.' He tipped the tea chest over, and files slid haphazardly out. Loose sheets escaped and Henry threw them on the heap. He took up a file, unclipped its contents and watched them shower down amongst the leaves, dirty paper and orange peel. 'Save the actual files. Just burn the paper.' There were shouts for him from the house, and he went off.

Claudia and Rod stood still, staring at the loose sheets covered with Henry's neat black writing underlined here and there in red. The flies buzzed over the rat's carcass. Claudia sighed, and picked up a piece of paper near her foot; it was a photocopy of two printed pages. She looked at it, then held it out and declaimed:

'"*After Richard had returned from Oxford to his father's house, he said one day to his sister, who loved him with real affection: 'My beloved sister, thou hast two tunics which I greatly covet, one white and the other grey. Therefore I ask thee if thou will kindly give them to me, and bring them tomorrow to the wood near by, together with my father's rain-hood'. She agreed willingly, and the next day according to her promise, carried them to the said wood, being quite ignorant of what was in her brother's mind.*" (No good, I'll be bound.) "*And when he had received them he straightaway cut off the sleeves from the grey tunic and the buttons from the white*" (that must have pleased his sister no end) "*and as best he could he fitted the sleeves to the white tunic. Then he took off his own clothes with which he was clad and put his sister's tunic next to his skin, but the grey, with the sleeves cut out, he put over it, and put his arms through the holes which had been*

119

cut; and he covered his head with the hood aforesaid, so that in some measure, as far as was in his power he might present a certain likeness to a hermit. But when his sister saw this she was astounded and cried: 'My brother is mad, my brother is mad.'" Good for her. Very suspicious beginning to the mystic life, I must say.' Claudia threw the sheet down, and picked up a file. Paper cascaded out. Rod held a file and hesitated.

'I really hate doing this.'

'He means it.'

'He'll regret it.'

'Possibly not, Rod. Come on, let's start the conflagration.'

They both bent down simultaneously, and cracked their heads together. Vision swimming, they put their arms round each other's shoulders and staggered about laughing.

'Ouch. I could have done without that. My thumb is bad enough.'

'Poor Claudia.' Rod stroked her forehead.

'Poor you.' She leant forward suddenly, and kissed the bumped place. 'Thanks for turning up today. It's going to be ghastly. This bonfire's just the beginning. You wait until you see Ma. She's demented already. She keeps going round moaning about how she wishes she'd planned the move better.' Claudia set light to the first pile of paper. 'Let's stay here as long as possible. I want to keep out of her way.'

But they were only half way through the burning when Di's voice was heard shouting, 'Claudia! I need you. Where are you, Claudia?'

'Oh, groans.'

They tipped the untouched files out of the packing case, and stood indecisively.

'Shall I go on burning this stuff?'

'No, you come too, I need moral support. We can do this later.'

Rod balanced the empty case on his head and followed her. There were crowds of people everywhere, mostly parishioners who had come to help. Di looked desperate, while Henry directed them cheerfully about.

'Now, Mrs Weatherall, I think the most valuable thing you could do would be to make tea for everyone . . .'

Removal men shuffled past carrying long heavy rolls of carpet and underfelt.

'Claudia, go and lay the carpet in your room.' Di tripped over a fender. 'Oh, this is chaos. Go on, go and do it; take Rod, anything, but just get it done before they put furniture into the house.'

'Right.' Claudia and Rod ran off thankfully, and found carpets being put down all over the new house. Josephine and Evelyn were upstairs laying a bedroom carpet, arguing between them.

'All the carpets are too big,' wailed Josephine to Claudia. 'These rooms are so tiny. I wish Ma had measured up more carefully. I'm going to fetch her.'

'Don't. It'll just make things worse. That looks like my carpet, Rod. Heave-ho.'

Between them they centred and unrolled it. As in the other rooms, the carpet flowed up the walls.

'By the time my bed and my furniture have gone in, there won't be room to move.' Claudia sat down despondently. 'Oh Rod, this house is awful.' Evelyn came in and started to do handstands against the wall. Then Di appeared to see how the carpet-laying was progressing; having seen she went away without saying anything except to stop Evelyn's handstands. Claudia and Rod went to help with the downstairs carpets. Henry breezed in carrying a precious vase, said: 'Well, all this looks very good' as he put the vase on a shelf, and then disappeared again. Claudia looked at Rod and raised her eyes to heaven.

The moment arrived for the grand piano to be moved. The legs were taken off, and five men manoeuvred it into the new house. It seemed to take up half the sitting room. A cabinet that was supposed to stand beside it would not fit in, and was taken out again. More and more furniture was brought over, would not fit in, and began to pile up outside. The front lawn of the new house looked like the higgledy-piggledy prelude to an auction.

'Let's sell it all,' said Claudia. She was sitting on a chest of drawers eating a sandwich; everyone had stopped for lunch, and Di had brought a picnic basket over for her family. Di herself was now lying on the large sofa (brought over by mistake) with her eyes shut. 'Let's have our own private auction.'

'Most of this will get in with a bit of rearrangement,' said Henry.

'You must be joking.' Di sat up. 'There's no room for any more. No *room*, Henry.'

'No need to shout, dearest.'

'So what are we going to do?'

'Sell it all.'

'Shut up, Claudia. I don't want all our nice family things to be gone for ever.' Josephine sounded surprisingly upset.

'Store it then.'

'If we sell it, it's gone for ever. Then one day when we're all grown up we might be sorry.'

'You really mind about it, don't you, Jo.' Di held out a hand to her daughter, but Josephine ignored it.

'Yes, I do.'

'Well, for the moment this stuff will have to go back into the big house until we decide what's to be done.' Henry went into the new house to inspect its full-ness. Josephine took another sandwich gloomily.

'Why did they have to build it so *small*? When I practise the piano I'm going to deafen everyone.'

'Now we've moved you'll have to give up the piano, of course.'

'Claudia, you're a beastly tease.'

'Evelyn will have to give up her brilliant indoor gymnastic displays.'

'And you'll have to give up being a pig.'

122

Then it began to rain; big drops spattered on the polished wood of the chests, the large carved sideboard, the glass-fronted bookcase (four inches taller than the new ceilings). Frenzied activity now took place outside the new vicarage: the removal men threw protective blankets over the furniture, Henry shouted instructions, people dashed about. Then the rain became a downpour; teams of people tottered with heavy loads back to the old house. The trampling of many feet made the garden look like a muddy playing field; the inside of the half-empty house became covered in wet earth, and smelt pungently of wet wool as the soaked blankets were whipped off the furniture again.

'Bugger possessions,' muttered Claudia as a heavy piece of furniture caught her shin. 'Bugger the rain.'

'My dusters and cloths, what did I do with them? Quick, dry the rain off those surfaces.' Di rushed about. Claudia went and dragged down the clothes still on the kitchen drier and began to use them. Rod found himself rubbing down a table with a petticoat and tights. He caught Claudia's eye, and they both started to laugh uncontrollably.

'I wish I could see the funny side.' Di smiled wanly at them. 'The rain is the final straw. Oh hateful, hateful day! Why did we ever agree to leave this dear house—'

'We didn't actually have much choice.' Henry took her arm. 'Come on, Di, you're needed in the other house. No one knows where to put things without you.'

The rain poured down; mud was carried in everywhere; boxes of china and glass were left outside because they could not spoil; water collected in upturned cups; Rod saw Henry pick one up and drink the contents.

'Rod, dear boy, I'm sure you've had enough. Do stop. You've been wonderful.'

'I'll have to go at five.'

'Why don't you stop now? We're through the worst. The men are off very soon.'

123

'I'll wait till five. I'm not on duty until half past.'

'You did finish burning my files, didn't you? It's such a relief to know it's done.'

'Lucky we started it before the rain came.'

A few minutes later Rod hurried down to the bonfire; scattered around were the unburnt, sodden files. Afraid Henry would find them, he collected them up and stacked them under a yew tree. He then went and joined Claudia in the old kitchen, where she was making tea for the removal men.

'Those files are wet through—unburnable now.'

'Files? Oh, help. We never finished.' Claudia leant against the draining board, dirty and tired. She cradled her sore thumb. Rod put his arm round her, and she relaxed against him in her tiredness. The kettle boiled unheeded.

'Today's cataclysmic, isn't it? We're like Noah and his family trying to fit into an ark. Dad's very like Noah.' She sighed. At that moment the Daltons' cat jumped on the draining board and miaowed loudly. 'You're just in time for embarkation.' Claudia laughed as she stroked the cat.

'Where's the tea for the men?' Di hurried in. 'Come on Claudia, they're nearly ready to go. Follow me,' she called over her shoulder, and the five men came into the kitchen. All except one lit cigarettes; there was an atmosphere of jovial unease as tea was drunk. The cat leapt on the kitchen table and sat on a pile of underwear—bras and briefs rejected as being no use for drying furniture.

'The cat's not going to like its new home.'

'It's not the only one.'

After a while the men left, and Di said to Rod: 'When are you off?'

'In five minutes.'

'I really meant, leaving Yorkshire?'

'After the cabaret, I suppose.'

'Well, please camp here if you want to—you'd be very welcome if you'd like a few more days up north. Just choose any room, we can lend you a camp bed.'

'I might take you up on that offer.'

'I mean it. Do.'

As they talked, Claudia wandered away into the dining room. Di went up close to Rod.

'Did you really burn all Henry's notes?'

'Most of them. The rain has spoiled the rest.'

'I wish he hadn't wanted that done today of all days.'

'We tried to stop him. He was determined. He even seemed happy about it.'

'He probably was. He's enjoyed all this. I didn't really believe him when he said possessions didn't matter to him. I believe him now.'

'What do you believe, dearest?'

'That possessions don't matter to you.'

Henry, filthy and drenched, smiled at her. He looked through the adjoining door into the dining room at the large articles of furniture standing haphazardly around. 'How undignified they all look. Very ruffled about their indecorous treatment. I think we should sell them, not store them, I honestly do.'

'I suppose so.'

'Goodbye, you pompous handsome lot, may you raise us an equally handsome sum.' He saw Claudia standing at the end of the room, gazing out of the window at the rain. 'We'll spend the money on a good holiday. We'll all go to Greece next year, or Italy. How about that, Claudia my love?'

She turned round from the window, and they saw that her eyes were streaming tears.

Plaisir d'amour ne dure qu'un moment
Chagrin d'amour dure toute la vie.

The joys of love are but a moment long,
The pain of love endures the whole life long.

Your eyes kissed mine, I saw the love in them shine,
You brought me heaven right then when your eyes kissed
   mine.

My love loves me, and all the wonders I see,
A rainbow shines in my window, my love loves me.

And now he's gone, like a dream that fades into dawn,
But the words stay locked in my heartstrings, my love
   loves me.

Hell, I'm going to sing that on Saturday. It's corny, but what do I care. Rod will curse at a new song. I'll sing it unaccompanied, that's what I'll do; it'll be stronger that way. And if Gerry doesn't come I don't care, I don't care, I'll be singing for myself.

I'll have to go over to the new house soon; it's after midnight. The acoustic in this room is so good now it's empty. Oh the blissful peace and quiet. What a day. Let me sing Plaisir again, and make the whole place echo.

'Claudia? What are you up to?'

'Singing.'

'I realize that. But why now—you'll never be up by seven at this rate. You must come to bed.'

'Yes, Ma. I'm coming. Just five more minutes. I'm going over the cabaret songs.'

'I'm glad you're doing Plaisir d'Amour. Such a lovely old tune. La-laa, laa, laaa—'

'I'll come now. I've lost the mood.'

Horrid new house. Horrid kitchen. Horrid narrow staircase. Horrid, horrid bedroom. Life isn't fair at the moment. Everything I love is taken away. Ma keeps putting her arm around me. I wish she wouldn't. There's nothing she can do at the moment, nothing. The only person who helps at all is Rod.

'How's your hand, darling?'

'Still painful.'

'Today can't have done it much good. Let me look. Poor love. A clean bandage, I think.'

'At least I've been too busy to think about it. 'Night, Ma.'

It feels very early. Half five. Damn. No shutters, no curtains— the light must have woken me. I'll never get to sleep again. Hey-ho for the windmills of the mind. Gerry, Gerry, Gerry. If only I could cut my feelings right out of myself, cauterize myself. His face is so attractive, his hands, the way he talks— don't, don't. Plaisir d'amour . . . I'm going to get up. What shall I wear today? Sackcloth and ashes, sackcloth and ashes. Now, let's organize this pigsty a little. I can't find anything.

'You've woken me up.'

'Sorry, Jo. I was trying to be quiet. I didn't think I'd disturb anyone.'

'The walls are made of paper. I'm going to get into your bed.'

'What's wrong with your own?'

'I didn't make it properly last night and it's come apart. Wasn't yesterday dreadful?'

'Where shall I put my picture of the girl on the river bank? I do love her so.'

'Sh. We must whisper. Above the bed.'

'Perhaps.'

'What do you think we're really going to do with all that furniture?'

127

'Sell it.'

'I can't bear the thought.'

'Don't be so sentimental.'

I wish I hadn't cried so much with Gerry. He hates people crying. So do I. I should have kept my cool. Perhaps he wouldn't have been so final with me then. Oh God, God.

'Do answer me, Claudia.'

'What?'

'I said, do you like Rod a lot?'

'I think he's the nicest person I've met in a long time. There's only one thing wrong with him.'

'What?'

He's not Gerry.

'What, what? Tell me.'

'Never you mind, nosy-Jo.'

'Beast. Anyway, Evelyn says he's in love with you. She's sure.'

'Bully for her. If you could stir yourself out of that bed and help me move this bookcase under the window, I'd get on quicker.'

'Claudie, what's going to happen next year?'

'Much the same as this year. Breakfast, lunch and dinner; Harvest, Christmas and Easter.'

'I meant to you—will you stay on and take your exams again?'

'I'll have to. I did so badly. I'm a fool. I know I can do well. I could kick myself.'

'Dad said a setback like this might do you good.'

'Thanks very much. He would.'

'What would you do after university?'

'Let me get there first. Why all these questions, anyway?'

'I don't know. I just felt like asking. When I saw you yesterday with Rod, I thought perhaps you'd get married to him one day.'

'Don't make me laugh.'

*

128

Thank goodness the job is ending soon. Two more days only. I feel really fed up with it now. Dick, Kevin, Rod, even though I like them all I've had enough of the whole set-up. And Nora, shrewd old Nora. Off she goes until next year again. I do sometimes wonder whether she loves Dad. Something brings her back to this part of the world. I'm tired of this bike-ride too. I suppose it would be marginally worse if it was uphill going home.

'Morning, Claudie love. How did the great move go?'

'Ghastly, Nora. Really awful.'

'Go on, tell.'

'There was total confusion. Ma hadn't measured anything properly. Half our furniture won't fit in. The carpets practically cover the windows. The rain didn't help. It was like a Marx brothers film, with muddy wet people carting stuff back and forth.'

'Poor Di. She really dreaded it. I think that's why she kept putting off planning it.'

'It was worse than she expected. What sort of eggs are they having for breakfast?'

'Fried, with bread. Do the bread.'

'Right.'

'Rod came back exhausted yesterday.'

'He kept me sane. Half or a whole piece each?'

'Half. How did your outing to Richmond with that Gerry go, by the way?'

'Fantastic, thanks. This fat is a bit stale.'

'You don't sound over the moon about it. What's wrong?'

'Shall I chuck the fat out?'

'It'll last two more days. So don't tell me.'

'There's nothing to tell.'

11

During their final Friday, the boys at King's Thornton were irrepressible. They made apple-pie beds, they constructed booby traps on the tops of doors, they faked accidents and invented telephone messages. Food flew around the dining room, table-tennis balls were fired from home-made pressure guns. But the final joke of the day outclassed all the others.

Rod had organized the evening's entertainment. He had put together various simple sketches—the most popular being *A Day in the Kitchen* involving the use of ludicrous ingredients for mad dishes, ably acted out by Nora and Claudia. Every joke was greeted with groans and screams of joy by the boys. Claudia and Rod sang a couple of songs to raucous appreciation and chorus. Hero though he was to them, the boys gave Rod a suspiciously enthusiastic ovation when the evening was over. Exhausted by the din, Rod retired to bed soon after the entertainment ended.

When he reached the top landing, he had to fumble his way to his door because the light bulb had gone. He found the handle, turned it and pushed ready to throw his guitar on the bed. But his door opened oddly, with a curious rustling resistance. His own light did not work either, and he stepped forward apprehensively in total darkness. He met a flimsy wall, a crackling cloud of paper, round him, above him, everywhere. He put a hand out and moved it blindly, taking a few steps forward. Paper. Newspaper, each sheet lightly screwed up, was filling his room like night fog. For a moment he wanted to scream at the strangeness of it. He moved to the left, and felt his bed against his shin. He eased the guitar down through the paper.

Laughter suddenly broke out behind him, and torches shone through the darkness. Gleeful boys pressed up to Rod's door to see the effect of the practical joke. His angry face peering through the clouds of newspaper caused the mirth to increase.

'You little devils. I'll murder the lot of you.' Rod came flailing out of his room. One or two boys fled, but more and more came past them to view the amazing sight. They flung themselves into the newspaper as if it were hay, and disappeared in a writhing tangle of shrieks. Dick and Nora came up to see what the noise was about, and laughed too.

'What a brilliant idea,' said Dick. 'I wonder which of the little fiends thought of it.'

Rod was less amused. 'They can bloody well clear it up.'

'Put the light on.'

'The bulb's gone.'

'I'll get one, there's some up here in the cupboard.' Nora fumbled for one.

'Right, you boys. Joke's over now. Find the window and push the paper out.' Dick fell over a chair as he felt his way across the room. 'Come on, you lot. Start passing the stuff to me.' He bundled armfuls out, and the rumpled sheets floated down into the garden and bounced across it in the wind, cartwheeling along through the darkness.

'Some of you go down and collect that paper so that it can be burnt. We don't want it all over the garden.' Nora switched the light on and then went and put an arm round Rod. 'You look fagged out. Come down to my sitting room and have a cup of something nice while these horrid wicked boys clear up the mess.'

Rod followed Nora; his legs felt like lead he was so exhausted; he wanted to stretch himself out to sleep anywhere, in the corridor, anywhere. He cursed the boys. Some of them must have done it during the evening's entertainment. He hadn't noticed anybody missing except for Kevin, who had cried off taking part.

131

As he went into Nora's room he saw Claudia putting up a camp bed.

'Hi. Thought you'd gone.'

'I decided it was ridiculous to go home now when I have to be back by seven-thirty. Anyway I think I would have fallen off my bike I'm so tired.'

'Me too.'

Nora appeared with a saucepan of warm milk and three mugs containing chocolate powder. She told Claudia about the newspaper-filled room.

'What a zany idea. You should have called me to look at it.'

'Quite enough people came to look at it.'

'Oh, Rod, you must have felt as if you'd walked into another world.'

'It was weird for the first few minutes. Weird. Particularly since the little sods had removed the light bulbs.'

'It's a fabulous idea. I wonder who thought of it.' Outside, amid shouting, three boys under the direction of Kevin were starting a bonfire of newspaper. After watching them for a few minutes as she sipped her chocolate, Claudia added: 'I bet it was Kevin.'

'Could be.'

'He probably got a few of the boys to help.'

Boys ran up with grey armfuls, and these were held down on the flames by Kevin wielding a long pole. He looked as if he was enjoying himself. The newspaper flared up and quickly died down; the fitful fire was a slightly macabre sight.

'Burning paper seems to be part of life at the moment.' Claudia yawned.

'I'm sure Kevin wouldn't do a thing like that,' said Nora. 'Anyway, what does it matter. It was a good joke.'

'I'm going to bed.' Claudia took off her jeans and jersey, and in T-shirt and briefs slipped into a sleeping bag. 'Pass me that cushion, Rod, would you.' She tucked the cushion under her head; her hair flowed over it. 'What a week. I'll be a wreck for the cabaret tomorrow.' She shut her eyes and began humming

132

Plaisir d'Amour. Nora started to sing the song in a clear if tremulous soprano; Claudia promptly sang contralto, and Rod added a bass part. Nora started to waltz round the room holding an imaginary partner, singing as she danced.

'I love dancing. You'll dance with me tomorrow, Rod, won't you?'

'I'm a hopeless dancer.' But Nora took his hands and made him circle round the room with her. They were interrupted by yells and laughter below the window; with a sigh, Nora went off to investigate.

Rod stood by the window, his mind full of Claudia's firm white thighs. She lay with her eyes shut, her mat of hair hanging down over the end of the camp bed. He swallowed, longing to stroke her hair. A boy outside started to cry noisily.

'What can be going on?' If he just leant forward and casually touched her—

'I'm past caring.' Claudia turned on her side and pulled the sleeping bag closely up round her face. 'I've had it. Goodnight.'

'Goodnight.' He put his hand on her shoulder as he passed, but she gave no sign of having felt him. Stepping over her jeans and jersey, he left the room and pounded up the back staircase cursing himself for a useless inept fool. When he got to his room it was darkened and empty. He switched on the light, which revealed tatters of newspaper everywhere and an even greater confusion than there had been previously. Several things had been knocked to the floor and trodden on. His alarm clock was under the bed and no longer ticking. He shook it. Something tinkled loosely inside.

'Hell. Bloody hell.' He stripped and got into his distinctly grubby unmade bed, retrieving a rolled-up ball of newspaper as he did so. He fell asleep with the light on; hours later it woke him, and he stumbled out to switch it off. As he sank back into sleep, he heard cockerels crowing down in Thornton.

'I'm leaving with the boys,' announced Kevin at breakfast. It was the only thing he said to the others except goodbye. Rod

133

thought he looked very pleased with himself. The coachload left at midday; after the excited din of departure, the silence was eerie. Nora and Claudia went through the whole house stripping beds, dropping the linen down the stairwell into a huge heap in the hall. There were two vast wicker baskets to fill up; Rod was about to help, but Dick led him away.

'Woman's work,' he muttered.

'Don't let Claudia hear you.'

'I need your help with the final report. It's best done immediately while everything's fresh in our minds.'

They went into the common room, where Dick had spread his papers all over the large central table. The rest of the room, with its piles of dog-eared comics, tattered armchairs and worn rugs, looked dismal in the bright sunshine. There were ample, elegantly proportioned french windows which looked out over the playing fields; each window was hung with shiny green unlined curtains a good eighteen inches too short. Rod opened a window, and Dick's papers promptly danced everywhere in the chilly draught.

'Shut that damned thing. Never open windows in Yorkshire, it's always too cold or too windy. Or both.'

They settled down amicably and worked until Nora, her son Jimmy, and Claudia came in with a tray of food. As if to underline their imminent departure, they ate standing up, or perched on the arms of chairs. All except Jimmy, who sat on the floor with a comic.

'Come on, Claudia, give us the drill for this evening,' said Nora. 'I'm looking forward to a few high jinks.'

'You can go mad in the disco; they're having one in the cellar. Dad was against it, I can't think why.'

'I'll try anything.' The departure of the boys had invigorated her. 'What time's the cabaret?'

'About ten, I think.' She looked at Rod. 'We must be mad. I feel sick at the thought.'

'I'm deliberately not thinking.'

Claudia went and opened a window, and again Dick's

papers flew about. He gave an anguished yell. 'Sorry, Dick, it felt so stuffy in here.'

'I hate writing this report, and you're all in league to stop me.'

'Well, I'm off before you murder me. Unless you still need me, Nora me old darlin'—' Claudia rubbed her dirty face with her equally dirty hands. 'I can't wait to soak in a bath.'

'Off you go. You're the prima donna tonight.'

Rod followed Claudia down the long echoing corridors to the kitchen. 'I hate to nag you, Claudia, but we really ought to have a run-through of our programme.'

'Help. Yes. I've got to the point of praying tonight will never arrive. Come down as soon as you're packed and ready. Ma's expecting you.' She pushed her bike out and looked round at the deserted gardens. 'I'm glad this session's over. It's been a hard stint, somehow. See you.' She bicycled off. Rod watched her until she was out of sight, and then wandered across the lawn. He was full of the sense of melancholy which the ends of enterprises bring.

He sat down on one of the low parapet walls which in days of earlier splendour had overlooked an intricate rose garden, terraces of lawns, and a small ornamental lake. Now only the lawns remained; the lake itself had been filled in to form a second games pitch, on which birds were peacefully feeding. He watched them, not knowing what they were. He looked at the trees around him, and wondered how many he could name. Oak, sycamore, elm, cedar; he could go no further with certainty. The whole estate was full of unusual trees planted by the Thorntons. He had been here four weeks and hardly looked at them; his life had been dominated by his involvement with people, Claudia above all. Perhaps if he had time today he would walk round the grounds; it seemed a waste not to—

'Rod! Rod!' Nora shouted from a window above him. 'Give me a hand to move this bed.'

The birds down on the pitch rose in alarm at her voice. Rod sighed and went in. Sod the work. He had had enough.

135

It was late afternoon by the time he had packed up his kit and walked down to the Daltons'. Claudia was actually looking out for him, and hurried him into the empty sitting room of the old house.

'I'm beginning to panic. I need a good rehearsal to calm me down.' She took a sheet of paper from the mantelpiece. 'How about this for our running order. By the way, I forgot to tell you, I'm adding *Plaisir d'Amour*—unaccompanied. Do you mind?'

'It's your show, Claudia. Of course I don't.'

'Let's do a proper run through from start to finish, then we can see where the weak parts are.'

'Suits me.' Rod tuned his guitar and they began.

They had hardly finished the first song when Di stuck her head through the door. 'That's where you are. Hullo, Rod. Come on both of you, it's teatime, proper high tea to give you energy for this evening—'

'Oh for goodness' sake, Ma, we don't need food *now*. We've only just started, and we've got the whole programme to go through. Leave something out for us, we'll come over later.'

'Calm down, Claudia, there's no need to shout at me.' Di withdrew.

'Honestly, mothers.' Claudia took a deep breath, and started to sing again. She was in excellent voice; Rod was gripped with excitement as he played. Her high notes were true and secure, her low notes rich and unforced, her middle register equally firm. Her passage from register to register was sometimes rough and her breath control was haphazard, but good teaching would rectify all that.

'I keep saying it, but your voice is fantastic.'

'This acoustic's so good.'

'It's not just the acoustic.'

'I do so love singing.'

'I suppose that technically you're a mezzo-soprano, aren't you?'

136

'It sounds silly, but I don't really know yet. They made me sing alto parts at school, although I longed to be with the sopranos.'

'Typical. You've got super high notes—I'm sure you're a sop with a good lower range. I'll tell you something else—I get the impression your voice has improved in the last four weeks.'

Claudia walked to the window and gazed out before replying. 'If it has, it's entirely due to you. You've encouraged me; nobody else ever has. I'm beginning really to believe in my voice. I've started to think of it almost as a separate part of me—like an extra dimension.'

'Sing me *Plaisir d'Amour*. That's the only thing we haven't gone through. I'm longing to hear it.'

She turned and gave him a half smile. 'No. You'll hear it this evening; that's soon enough. Besides, my voice is getting a bit tired. Come on, let's go and have something to eat.'

They jumped over flowerbeds through a squall of rain. 'Lovely weather again. I've forgotten what the sun looks like.'

Henry met them at the kitchen door. For a moment Rod did not recognize him; his hair was cut and flattened down; he was wearing a dark suit, white shirt and scarlet tie. Claudia wolf-whistled as she passed him.

'Hullo, gorgeous.'

'You two will have to get a move on, you know. I'm leaving now; it's seven already.'

'Don't fuss, Dad. You said the cabaret wouldn't be till ten o'clock, so it doesn't matter if we're not there at the beginning.'

'I don't trust you, Claudia. Rod, get yourselves there by nine at the very latest, won't you. Miss Topham's car is outside. I think she's insane to lend it to you, but there we are. It is at least fully insured.' Henry ran his hands through his hair and it promptly stood up on end again. He took a deckle-edged ticket out of his pocket and handed it to Rod. 'That'll get you both in.'

'Oh by the way Dad, we'll need another double ticket for Dick and Nora. I meant to tell you they were coming.'

'Claudia, you are the limit! I haven't got another ticket. They're completely sold out. There's been an excellent response this year.'

'But they're expecting to come.'

'You should have warned me in time.'

'They'll be dreadfully disappointed, Nora especially. Please, Dad. Can't something be done?' Claudia gave Rod a hot dog, and bit into one herself.

'You are too casual by half.' Henry stormed off upstairs, shouting that he was already late. He returned within a few minutes with a signed note stating that Rod and Claudia were the cabaret. Claudia muttered thanks as Henry rushed out of the kitchen again, shouting for Di. The front door slammed.

Josephine drifted into the kitchen. 'What are you two going to wear for this famous cabaret?'

'We're doing it in the nude, to give the locals a real thrill.'

'Oh, yeah. Don't bother to tell me. I'm not really interested.'

'Good. I'll save my breath for my singing.'

'No, but what *are* you going to wear?'

Rod laughed. 'I'm just as much in the dark as you are, Josephine. Let's wait and see what she's cooked up.'

Claudia disappeared upstairs. When she finally returned she was dressed in tight black trousers and a voluminous green silk shirt bound round the waist with tasselled cord. She had teased her hair into a wild halo round her head, and her eyes were heavily made up with iridescent green shadow. She held out a pair of black trousers and a black sweater to Rod; over her arm was a multicoloured silk jacket.

'Try on the trousers. They're Dad's. He won't mind. The sweater's mine—it's a loose one.'

Both trousers and sweater fitted adequately; then Claudia opened out the beautiful jacket. 'That's Ma's Hong Kong special—she must be mad to lend it to you—' began Josephine.

'It's all right. Rod isn't going to tear it—he'll only wear it for the cabaret.' It looked surprisingly effective, and not in the least effeminate.

138

'Does it really look O.K.?'

'Terrific. Honestly. Take it off again now, in case it gets wet.'

'I'll go and fetch my guitar and the music.'

'Good idea.'

When Rod had gone, Claudia hissed at Josephine: 'I didn't ask Ma, but it'll be too late to object by the time she sees it on stage.'

'You are dreadful.'

'If Rod knows I've borrowed it without her permission he won't wear it; he's such a fusspot over things like that. So shush.'

'You look amazing. Quite awful really.'

'Thank you, dear sister. Just the kind of pleasant encouragement I need.' Rod returned and they went to the front door.

'Hey, Evelyn. Come and take a look at Claudia.'

Evelyn shouted from upstairs. 'I have. Once is enough.'

'Goodbye, you charming pair of sisters. Be good.'

Please God, don't let Gerry be at the dance. I wish I hadn't asked him. But he said Dad had given him a ticket . . . perhaps he won't use it. Just the sight of him will throw me, I know it will.

I won't let it. There. If I'm going to be a professional, the wrong faces in the audience shouldn't upset me. Courage, Claudia. Don't let him see any more that he upsets you.

'Does my driving make you nervous?'

'What? No, Rod, of course not. Why should it?'

'I saw you clenching your hands like someone about to say stop, let me out, I'm terrified—'

'Don't be silly. I wouldn't know if you were driving badly anyway. I really must learn how to drive.'

'It's fun.'

'Dad isn't too keen on letting me loose in his car. Not that I blame him either. I hardly inspire confidence.'

Confidence. That's what I need for this evening, and at the moment I wish I was driving to Timbuktu. Well, at least Rod is one of those people who supports you, rather than undermining you like others I can think of. Perhaps Gerry was right; he would only harm me in the long run. I just wish the short run wasn't so unpleasant.

12

They picked up Dick and Nora, leaving Jimmy alone at King's Thornton with a list of telephone numbers in case of emergency. Nora was concerned about this arrangement, Jimmy cheerful. He had preferred to be on his own rather than join the younger Daltons at the vicarage.

Nora was dressed in a blue caftan which had been made for her by the under-matron at Elsted House School. It looked very good on her, and brought out the reddish tints in her hair. She had made herself up with care for once; indeed the only thing to spoil the effect of her get-up was her shoes. They were flat sensible brown leather sandals. She saw Claudia looking at them.

'Yes, I know. But I've nothing else with me, so they'll have to do. Rod, your Mum just rang. She wanted to know your movements, so I gave her the Daltons' number and she said she'd ring you there tomorrow.'

'Oh. Yes.' His home and family seemed remote. 'I don't know my plans yet.' He hoped Claudia would make some comment, but she said nothing. They all piled into the Mini, Dick in the back with Claudia.

'Whose car is this? You'd better not drink much then, Rod. The old girl might not appreciate any dents.' Dick looked very scrubbed and tidy beside Claudia's wild appearance.

'I'll do without alcohol; I'd prefer to keep to soft drinks.'

'You're so good, Rod.' Claudia dug at his shoulder blades. 'Too good to be true sometimes. Surely a glass of wine won't hurt you.'

'I'm not being *good* as you put it; I'm pleasing myself. I don't much like alcohol; I'll play better and drive better without it, so what's the hassle?'

'That's right, you stand up for yourself.' Nora tapped his knee. 'She's always getting at people. You keep her in order.'

'Don't be silly, Nora, no one can keep me in order. I am the unique Claudia Dalton, answerable to no one, didn't you know?'

'Pride comes before a fall.'

'I've fallen already.'

'Why don't we talk about a nice safe topic like the weather, or education, or—or—pot-holing, anything rather than argue.' When they all laughed at his remark, Dick protested: 'No, I mean it. Actually, I've always wanted to know about pot-holing.'

'You should have asked Kevin,' said Nora.

'No, really, did he do it?'

'Very keen. He didn't let on to the boys. I told him not to. I knew what would happen if he had. More little boys lost.'

'Horrible sport,' shuddered Claudia. 'Imagine squeezing your way in the dark along a narrow passage hundreds of feet below ground—ugh. Rod, turn right here. Sorry, should have warned you. The house is about five miles further along this side road.' As Rod braked suddenly and swerved to the right, his guitar shot off Claudia's knees and twanged ominously.

'Hey, watch it! That guitar's precious. Do give me more warning, Claudia, I can't possibly drive safely if you suddenly say turn right when we're practically past the turning.'

'Sorry, sorry, sorry.'

They drove on in silence for a while. Then Nora and Dick started to discuss the report he had finally finished. Suddenly Claudia screeched: 'That was the drive!'

Rod swore, slowed down and backed carefully. The empty drive looked very uninviting. 'Are you sure?'

'No. Now I look at it, I'm not. I seem to remember there was a huge cedar by the gate—'

'No cedar.'

142

'Let's go on. I know the house is near here, very near.'

'Wouldn't they have a notice up?'

'I don't know. Oh, despair.'

They crawled on for another mile, but there was no drive, only farm tracks. They went a little way down one of them and nearly stuck in mud. It was raining gently. Rod stopped the car when they were back on the road.

'Are you sure we're going in the right direction?'

'Absolutely.'

Dick groaned. 'Then where is this bloody place? I wish I hadn't come.'

A car was approaching. Nora leapt out and stood waving her arms in the middle of the road. The occupants of the car were clearly also going to the dance, and gave them directions. Everyone cheered up and within a quarter of a mile they came to a drive with a huge cedar, on which was pinned a notice saying DANCE and a bunch of balloons.

The drive was cripplingly bumpy, and the guitar twanged again as it hit the side of the car. All four climbed thankfully out when they reached the muddy temporary car park; the rain, fortunately, had stopped. Nora stepped backwards into a puddle and got mud all over one foot. She cleaned it up with a bunch of leaves.

'We *are* a motley group,' she muttered as they wandered over to the front door. 'They probably won't let us in.'

Claudia sailed up to the elderly man at the door, and presented her letter while Dick handed in the ticket and sidled past with Nora.

'Ah, the *cabaret*. We have put a small room at your disposal—up the stairs, turn left, you can't miss it.'

Rod and Claudia found a door bearing the notice: 'Reserved for the Cabaret', at which Claudia giggled. The room was a small untidy study; someone had put a tray with orange juice and glasses on the desk. Rod put his guitar beside it.

'They might have supplied us with champers as well.' Claudia's eyes glittered. 'Come on, let's get the feel of the party.'

Downstairs, the sound of the disco in the cellar made the house throb. The more sedate dancers were supplied with a marquee in which a small band was playing Glen Miller tunes. Good, tasty-looking food was laid out on tables in various rooms, and there seemed to be a copious supply of wine.

'Despite the bourgeois set-up, this is a good do,' said Dick when the four of them had looked around. 'Come on, Nora, let's feed first. I'm famished.'

'We'll eat after the cabaret.' Rod and Claudia left them to it, and went down to the disco. This had the obligatory strobe lighting and deafening music. There were about a dozen couples dancing.

'Let's dance now before it gets too crowded,' shouted Claudia.

A crowd would hide the inadequacy of his dancing, so he said, 'Later'.

'*Now*, you old stick in the mud.' She launched herself out onto the floor; she danced well, rhythmically, with her own combination of grace and energy. Rod jigged about near her, hoping his efforts did not seem too pathetic. But Claudia hardly noticed him; she danced with her eyes half-closed in the pleasure of movement. Rod found after a while that he too was dancing better; Claudia's precise sense of rhythm made it easy for him to answer her steps. He grinned at Claudia, but she was lost in her world.

Then behind her, framed in the doorway, he saw the man who had been with her in Ripon. He missed the beat, almost stopped dancing. The man was looking for someone, yet when he saw Claudia he turned and left after another quick glance around.

Rod's dancing was half-hearted now and he said: 'Let's stop and find a drink.'

But Claudia had moved towards someone else, a boy she knew who had been hovering without a partner. She waved at Rod. 'Fetch me a Coke— I can't bear to stop yet.'

144

'The hell I will.' Rod left her in the disco, and went to find Dick and Nora. This turned out to be a waste of time, because Nora was dancing with Henry, and Dick had found a ginger-bearded man with whom he was heatedly discussing Marxism. Rod left them to it, and went out on the terrace. Apart from Di, also dancing, there was nobody he knew. Couples wandered about on the terrace; Rod felt painfully lonely. He sat down on a bench and stared at the end of the sunset: shreds of dark cloud on a yellow and orange sky, lined with faint jet trails.

He could hear with equal clarity both the disco and the band; unable to bear the cacophony he got up and walked away from the house towards a sheltered geometric garden in the middle of which was a seat. He stretched out on this with his eyes shut. Scents of many different plants were strong all round him; he was in the middle of a formal herb garden. He reached out and picked a leaf; roundish, soft, and hairy, it smelt spicily of lemon. He bruised it with his fingers and put it on his forehead, then picked several more and laid them all over his face.

'Rod? Are you all right?' Henry stood at the edge of the herb garden. Rod sat up quickly, the leaves slipping off his face.

'Of course. I was wallowing in the nice smells of this garden.'

Henry approached round the neatly laid out beds. 'It's a famous herb garden—it contains a lot of rarities, though I'm not botanist enough to tell you which they are.'

'What's this called?' Rod picked up a lemon-scented leaf and held it out.

'Oh, that. Lemon balm. It's practically a weed it's so rampant. It's been planted near the seat because it can be picked with impunity by idle fingers.'

Rod laughed. 'And I thought it was something very special.'

'Well, it is, in its way. Come on, come inside and let me introduce you around. I don't suppose Claudia made any efforts in that direction.'

'Well, not really. I left her leaping about in the disco.'

The sun had now set, and someone had lit lanterns in the

trees and shrubs near the house. Rod did not particularly want to go in and talk to strangers, but Henry introduced him to a group of people and left him to make stilted conversation. Rod kept an eye on the crowd for Claudia, but there was no sign of her. Then he heard someone say that the cabaret was due to start soon, and panic flooded him. He hurried down to the disco but could not find Claudia there or anywhere else. Eventually he went in despair to the reserved room. There was Claudia with two young men, another girl and a bottle of wine.

'Rod! I looked for you. Join us—Edward, give him a glass of wine.'

'The cabaret is due to start soon.' He sounded prim and damping. Claudia gazed at him in alarm, her exhilaration evaporating.

'I don't believe it. Everybody out, quick. We must have peace and quiet.' She pushed her friends out of the door, ignoring their complaints. To his horror, Rod heard Edward calling out from the head of the stairs: 'Cabaret. Cabaret. Take your places for the cabaret.'

'Silly fool. I wish he'd belt up. There's still twenty minutes to go, if the time Henry gave us is right.' Rod banged the door shut. Claudia was standing in the middle of the room with her eyes shut and her arms stretched above her head.

'Oh, Rod. Panic, panic.'

'Don't be stupid. Sit down and take some deep breaths. Have you been drinking wine?'

'Hardly any.'

'You look flushed.'

'Too much dancing.' Claudia flopped into the chair. 'I was on a high.'

'You're mad to exhaust yourself. Look, I'm going to get us two cups of black coffee, and while I'm away you've got to get your voice going. Do some exercises or something, get your cool back and your throat relaxed.'

'Yes, maestro.'

His desire to shake her melted as he hurried to fetch coffee.

146

When he returned he heard her singing simple exercises; she was standing again, with her hands on her rib-cage. She looked less frenetic. He handed her the coffee, and they drank it in silence.

'Thank you, Rod. I don't know what I'd do without you. Shall we go through our duet? I find it the toughest.'

Ten minutes later Henry put his head round the door. 'We're all ready when you are. Everyone's in the marquee. I'm sure it'll be an appreciative audience.'

'Give us two more minutes, Dad. We need to tidy ourselves up.'

'I'll wait for you downstairs.'

Claudia put the silk jacket on Rod, and tidied his hair. He liked the feeling of her hands on his head, and wished it could last longer. She then took out a plastic bag bulging with make-up, and repaired her eye-paint. Rod watched her fascinated as she held a magnifying mirror very close and worked with quick skilled movement. When his mother or his sisters put on make-up they dabbed; Claudia stroked, brushed, painted with delicate flicks.

'Right. That'll do.' She threw the bag into a chair. 'We're ready. Oh, Rod, I feel sick. I've never sung before such a large audience.'

'Get you in trim for Covent Garden.'

She put her arm through his and they set off towards the stairs. By half-way down, she was tightly holding his hand. Henry led them round the outside of the marquee to the small flap entrance at the end behind the bandstand. The buzz of talk and laughter coming through the canvas was immensely loud, as if the tent of fabric covering these few hundred people was a natural amplifier. Claudia's hand clamped on Rod's.

'I feel even sicker,' she whispered. 'I'd like to run very fast out of sight.'

Henry turned round before entering the marquee. 'I'll give you just a short introduction—unless you'd prefer to do it yourselves after all—'

'No, no. No.'
'Good luck, then, my dears.'
They followed him through the flap.

Beer cans all over the piano, chairs and music stands all over the place. Blast the band for being such tramps. We should have set it all up earlier. While Dad's talking we'll straighten it up a bit—good, Rod's got the idea too.

And breathe steadily, Claudia, breathe steadily. Remember that singer's face, all open and relaxed and yet controlled. Think of her all the time, remember her voice, that lovely steady column of sound just pouring out until you wanted to explode with the joy of hearing it . . . Many people have good voices, few know how to sing—but I almost know; by good luck and by accident and by whatever you like, I almost know . . .

13

'So, I present to you, Rod and Claudia.'

Henry swept his arm back; there was polite welcoming applause. Rod and Claudia bowed as Henry made his way into the audience. Rod settled himself on a stool with his guitar ready; Claudia faced her audience. As she looked at them, her whole manner became confident and quietly powerful.

'All our songs are about love. Most folk songs are, I suppose. Anyway, we've chosen as wide a variety as possible, some very familiar, some not so. If you know the choruses, please join in. I'm sure you'll know our first song, the old favourite *The Oak and the Ash*.'

Claudia moved closer to Rod, and waited for him to give her her cue. When he saw how calm she seemed, his nerves began to lessen too.

'*A North country maid up to London had strayed,*
Although with her nature it did not agree.
She wept and she sighed and bitterly she cried:
I wish once again in the North I could be.'

Some of the audience joined in the first chorus; by the end of the song participation was more energetic so that Claudia repeated the last verse with most people singing:

'*No doubt, did I please, I could marry with ease;*
Where maidens are fair, many lovers will come.
But he whom I wed must be North country bred,
And carry me back to my North country home.'

The audience applauded loudly, and Claudia laughed and winked at Rod. From that point on they could do no wrong. Claudia in performance was an uplifter of everyone near her;

Rod found that her extra sensitivity to his accompaniment made him excel himself. Their acid, bitter duet, which they sang third in the programme, went better than it had ever done before. When they finished singing it, there was a deep silence before the applause began. They followed it with lighter songs, until again Claudia changed the mood abruptly.

She moved away from Rod and stood facing half away from her audience. She put her hands up near her chin; such was her magnetism that the audience watched her as if under a spell. With her eyes shut, she sang the first verse of *Plaisir d'Amour* very softly, in French. Then she slowly turned and began to sing the rest of the song facing the audience, hands down now, her body very still; her unaccompanied voice seemed to float as it defined the long plaintive lines of melody. By the last verse, the tension she had created was palpable; the gentle flapping of the stretched canvas was the only sound besides Claudia's voice. As she repeated the final verse in French, she stared out over the heads of her audience, her whole body projecting the reality of love's pain. Yet she did not move and her vocal dynamics were minimal.

Rod sat with his head bent. He had never heard her sing this song and he knew as he listened to her that he was right. Her talent was beyond the ordinary, not only because she had a fine voice, but she was stimulated by an audience into giving the song more meaning than he had ever thought it had. He tried to lessen the strength of his emotional reaction by analysing Claudia's power, but at the end of her song he had to keep his head bent because he was near tears. If he had looked up, he would have seen he was not the only one.

The applause and shouts of *encore* went on and on; Claudia just stood, and finally lifted a hand for silence.

'On with the show. We're going to sing one everybody knows—come on, join in.'

Claudia opened her voice to a full raucous blues volume and launched into *Careless Love*. Rod's guitar was inaudible most of the time, everyone's singing was so loud. In the uproar of

151

applause and chatter when the song was over, Claudia muttered to Rod: 'We never thought about encores. They're bound to want one. Let's end the cabaret there, then we can sing our last song as an encore.'

'You're the boss.'

They both bowed again, Rod picked up his guitar, and led Claudia out through the flap. Roars of *encore* followed them. Outside, Claudia hugged Rod and laughed in joy. 'Isn't this fantastic!' There was rhythmic shouting and stamping in the tent. Voices were calling out: 'Come back, Claudia.'

They had chosen as their last a haunting song called *Fare Thee Well*; Rod was afraid that despite its aptness, the choice of a lyrical lament was wrong after the lusty uproar of *Careless Love*. He had written a special guitar introduction, and worked out a particularly subtle accompaniment. It would never be heard at all. Yes, it was a bad choice of song.

But he reckoned without Claudia. As soon as she went in, the noise increased. She stood absolutely still, waiting. Again, such was her effect on her audience that they simply fell silent and watched her. She nodded at Rod, who played his solo faultlessly. Then she began:

'Oh, fare thee well, I must be gone and leave you for a while
Wherever I go I will return, if I go ten thousand miles
If I go, if I go, if I go ten thousand miles.'

With the repetition of *if I go*, Claudia's voice soared upwards; Rod had heard several folk singers interpret this song, but none gave such a powerful suggestion of movement and distance, of the hurt of absence. By the time she had reached the last verse she once more had the audience in complete thrall:

'Oh, the rivers never will run dry, or the rocks melt with the sun,
I'll never prove false to the boy I love, till all these things be done,
Till all, till all, till all these things be done.'

She then bowed once, left the tent, and ran with Rod alongside the canvas as the audience continued to applaud wildly.

152

'They're calling for you, listen.'

'I'm not going back. Quick, let's hurry to the changing room before anyone catches us.' Driven by a desire to escape from the sounds of her first success, she flew upstairs with Rod in tow. She flopped down in the armchair, suddenly limp.

'We're a success.'

'*You're* a success. You sang fantastically, better than I've ever heard you before.'

'Really?'

'Really.'

'And you played well, you know.'

The door opened and in came Di. She kissed them both. 'You were both very good—I was amazed how good. So were other people—I heard one or two snide comments before the cabaret began, but you swept everyone before you. Well done!'

Rod was still wearing the silk jacket. Claudia saw her mother eyeing it, and promptly started to take it off him.

'I'd no idea my clothes would fit you so well, Rod.'

'I didn't think you'd mind, Ma.'

'Well, how could I mind after such a splendid performance? Come downstairs and meet your public.'

Claudia hesitated. 'In a minute.'

'Gerry's friend is particularly anxious to meet you.'

'Gerry's friend?'

'Oh, haven't you met her yet? Angela someone, she's a lecturer at York University.'

'I need five minutes' break. I'll be down soon.' She almost pushed her mother out of the door. She took a bottle of cleanser out of her toilet bag and smeared the stuff thickly over her face. 'Gerry didn't come to the cabaret.'

'Oh? His loss.'

Claudia rubbed her face vigorously with tissues until every trace of her make-up had gone. She had brushed her hair smooth, and twisted it up into a knot. She now looked quite different from the wild girl who sang; her clean face gleaming with the residue of the lotion and her tidy hair made her much

153

younger. Even her brown eyes seemed a different shape.

'Right. I'm famished. Let's go and eat.'

People were slow to recognize her, and she and Rod were digging into platefuls of food before strangers came up and congratulated her. To Rod's surprise, her usual confidence deserted her; she was unable to deal with compliments. She stood close to Rod and continued to eat her supper while people talked. When the opportunity came, she muttered: 'Let's escape to the disco and darkness.'

But as they eased their way to the basement entrance, Henry came up with a woman.

'Don't disappear down there yet, Claudia. Angela Barker wants to meet you.' He left them together.

'Hullo, Claudia. I'm a friend of Gerry's.' She shook Claudia's hand. She was striking: very tall, with tight curly grey hair and a young face. Her sophisticated green chiffon dress and her poise marked her out from most of the women around her. 'You sang magnificently.'

'Thanks.'

'No, I mean it. Quite out of the ordinary. Tell me, who teaches you?'

'No one.'

'How amazing. I find it hard to believe anyone untaught could perform so well.'

'I taught myself.' Claudia backed towards the disco.

'Please don't misunderstand me. I meant, it's marvellous that you should have got so far without help.' She caught Rod's eye. 'What do you think of her?'

'I keep telling her she's got a true voice.'

'That's precisely what she's got. A true voice.' Angela Barker stared speculatively at Claudia, who remained unresponsive. 'Look, I hope you don't think I'm interfering or presumptuous, but I've got a suggestion to make. Would you like a professional opinion on your voice from someone who was once an opera singer herself, and has taught singing for years? She's more or less retired now, but in her day she was quite a name,

154

both as a singer and later as a teacher. She still does a little teaching, I believe.'

Claudia did not reply until Rod said sharply: 'Claudia!'

'Yes, I would. Thanks. Where does she live?'

'York. I'll introduce you to her whenever you like—preferably fairly soon, before the university term starts, because I'll be more tied up thereafter. But you choose when.' She had done her best to charm Claudia, and was beginning to succeed when she added: 'Gerry can give me your address and phone number—dances are hopeless places for exchanges of information, aren't they? Then I can ring you to fix a time.'

At Gerry's name, Claudia withdrew. 'Fine.' She looked over her shoulder. 'If I don't go and dance now I shall explode.' She disappeared down the stairs to the disco. Angela Barker made a wry face at Rod.

'Persuade her it's a good idea, won't you? Oriana Donskova really knows about singing—I can't wait for her to hear Claudia.'

'I'll try.'

Gerry appeared, saying, 'I was looking for you, Angela.'

'I was talking to that amazing girl. You were a fool not to come and listen to her sing.'

'I have heard her before.'

'In that case it's even more surprising you didn't come and listen. She's special.'

'You know me—I'm a philistine about music—'

Rod melted away, and found Claudia dancing by herself downstairs.

'You were dreadful to that woman.'

'I didn't like her.'

'She's really serious about helping you.'

'Bully for her.'

'Don't be ridiculous—you must go and see this singing teacher in York.'

'Who said I wouldn't?' Claudia's sly glance met his. 'It still doesn't mean I have to like Ms Angela Barker. Hell, here she is.'

155

With Angela was Gerry. As they arrived, the music changed to a slow number, and couples put their arms round each other and shuffled. Claudia immediately put her arms on Rod's shoulders, and linked her hands behind his neck; controlling his surprise at this affection, he held her round the waist. A sense of perfect happiness flowed through him. He put his chin down on her hair, which smelt freshly washed. She turned her head to one side, and he realized then that she was looking for Gerry. Gerry and Angela, cheek to cheek (she was exactly his height), were dancing in a far corner. When Claudia saw them, her grip on Rod tightened.

'I heard Angela Barker telling Gerry he was a fool to miss your singing. He didn't look too pleased.'

'I don't care what he feels.'

But this was belied a few minutes later. The music changed to rock, and Gerry came up and tapped Rod on the shoulder. 'Excuse me, dear sir, but may I borrow this young firebrand for the next dance?' He took Claudia's hand; she smiled, her face suddenly alight. Rod swung away to the side of the room, his happiness obliterated. He saw Angela sitting alone, smoking, and turned away. Gerry was a good dancer, and from the complicated steps they were doing, he and Claudia had clearly often danced together. Rod could not help watching them. Claudia's eyes flashed as she danced; she and Gerry were talking when the steps permitted it. Then without warning, Rod saw her give Gerry a hard slap on the face. She came over to Rod in fury.

'Take me home.'

'—'

'*Take me home*. Please.' She grabbed Rod's arm and pulled him from the disco.

'Look, Claudia, what on earth are you up to?'

'I'm fed up with this dump. Let's go.' She hurried through the hall, heading for the main staircase. She passed her mother on the way, who tried unsuccessfully to intercept her.

'Claudia, come and meet—oh, drat the girl. Rod, what's

156

happened? Why is she in such a rage?'

'Er—nothing much really—'

'Well, just tell Claudia would you, if you can possibly get anywhere near her without being pulverized, that someone would like to engage her to sing at a dance next month, and she'd better come and meet him if she wants the job.'

'I think she's keen to go home—'

'What, already? How unlike her. Tell her not to be ridiculous. She can't go now—' Di was swept away by friends.

Oh, can't she. She'll walk if I don't take her. Rod stood hesitating at the foot of the stairs until a hand descended heavily on his shoulder.

'There you are,' said Dick. He leaned close. 'I've been looking for you. Nora's got a bit sozzled, and wants to go home. I think I've had enough myself—'

'You are all the limit. Claudia's throwing tantrums and wanting to leave, and now you two—I've had enough of the lot of you.'

'Hey, Rod, wait a minute.'

Dick followed Rod up to the dressing room, where they found Claudia banging about throwing clothes into a carrier bag. She scowled at Dick.

'What did you think of the cabaret?'

'I—er—well, I didn't actually get to it, you see I was talking to this ginger-haired guy and—'

'*Dick*. You traitor! My big moment and you miss it. What's the point of bringing friends.' Rod could see that she was talking for the sake of it. 'Mind you, Nora didn't miss the show. She had tears running down her face at the end of *Plaisir d'Amour*. I saw her.'

'Nora's a sentimental fool, currently lying very much the worse for wear on a sofa in the conservatory. Anything makes her cry—a choirboy only had to open his mouth the other night on telly, and she was off.' Claudia threw a cushion at Dick, who caught it and then stood absent-mindedly hugging it. 'She and I would like to go home.'

'So would I.'

'I think you're all a lot of killjoys. I'm just beginning to relax and enjoy myself.' Rod turned away to hide a yawn; in fact, he was profoundly tired, but in no mood to end the party. 'Oh, what the hell. I give up. Get yourself together, Claudia, and we'll go and find Nora.'

'I am got together.' Claudia would not look at him.

They found Nora in the conservatory with her sandalled feet on the arm of a sofa; she was snoring, her mouth slightly open.

'Let's sit on her.' Claudia was poised above her.

'Don't be mean. NORA!' Dick bellowed in her ear. Nora woke with a convulsive movement.

'Help. Yes? Oh, it's you. Nice dance.' She settled back again, closing her eyes.

'Nora, up you get. We're going.'

'Not yet. I'm so sleepy. Later.'

'Wake up, Nora. Or get yourself a lift home.' Rod was losing patience with all three. At that moment Di appeared in the door of the conservatory with a plump man in tow. She cried:

'There they are! The cabaret plus accomplices.'

'Nora's exhausted, so we're going home,' announced Claudia.

'Don't leave for my sake,' said Nora, opening her eyes again. 'I'm happy sleeping here.' She scratched a foot and settled herself more comfortably.

'This is Mr Fairweather, Claudia. He wants to book you to sing.'

Claudia gazed at Mr Fairweather, who jingled coins in his pockets as he explained that his Masonic Lodge were having a Wives' Evening dinner-dance in November and would Claudia like to give them a short entertainment?

'Not in term time. Sorry.'

'Oh, I had no idea you were still at school—' Mr Fairweather's coins danced harder.

'Claudia, I'm sure you could fit this in—'

'Ma, not in term time. I've got all those exams to re-take,

158

don't forget.' Claudia pinched Nora, who yelped and sat up, groaning. Mr Fairweather backed away, as if the motley group round the sofa were too much for him to cope with.

'Another time perhaps—'

'Oh, sure,' said Claudia airily; she could see that Mr Fairweather could not wait to escape. 'Yes, do try again. Goodbye, Mr Foulweather,' she ended when he had gone out of earshot.

'Claudia, you go too far.'

'Ma, I am absolutely *not* going to sing, ever, at a Masonic dinner-dance. So in the circumstances I think I handled him quite well.' She kissed her mother's cheek. ''Night. See you at breakfast. Or whatever.'

'You wait till you're on your own. You won't be so fussy where you sing,' said Nora, tottering and bleary-eyed. 'I know I look drunk but I'm not. I lay down after the cabaret for a little rest and I've been asleep ever since.'

Di put her arm round Nora and went with them to the car park. Rod stalked ahead, angry and depressed. He could hear Dick asking Di about the house and estate; who owned it, did they farm it themselves, etc. He sounded as if he was warming up for a denunciation of the capitalist system, but in fact when they were all settled in the car, he dozed off. Nora also was snoring again within minutes. Claudia was silent as Rod drove home; whenever he looked in the rear mirror, he could see her eyes glittering in the dark. At one point he said: 'Left or right here?'

'Left.' She sounded miserable.

After a while Rod went on: 'I feel flat too. For you it must be worse: after such an exhilarating triumph the sense of anti-climax is natural. Newton's Third Law: that action and re-action are opposite and equal.'

'Don't moralize.'

'That was physics, not morality.' There was silence again until they arrived at King's Thornton and with difficulty unloaded Nora and Dick. Rain had begun falling and the two crumpled figures ran unsteadily round the house. Rod did not see Dick again because he left early the following morning.

Rod drove quickly down to the vicarage, and parked outside the old house. He and Claudia sat on in the car from sheer inertia; rain trickled down the windows. Rod still felt angry; the image of Claudia's hand hitting Gerry's face repeated itself in his mind, and the gesture sickened him. Di was right. She went too far. He got out of the car, and waited for Claudia to ease herself out from the back.

'My guitar.'

'Oh, yes.' She passed it out.

'I haven't got a key. Is the back door unlocked?'

'I don't know. Probably not. I'll come with you.' She followed him down the path, ignoring the rain. She felt under a nearby stone and retrieved a key, and they unlocked the heavy front door. Their footsteps thundered on the bare boards. Rod expected Claudia to leave with her usual brusqueness; indeed for once he would have been relieved if she had. Instead she accompanied him into the long sitting room where a camp bed had been made up. She closed the wooden shutters quickly.

She still did not leave. Piles of music had been left on the mantelpiece; she wandered over and flipped through the sheets. 'Josephine's stuff.' Rod hovered uneasily; there was nowhere to sit. Claudia leant against the mantelpiece, her face tense. Suddenly she burst out: 'Oh, I am such a fool. I wish I hadn't made Gerry come to the dance.'

'I've no doubt he feels the same.'

'I went on nagging him to come.' She turned and rested her forehead on the mantelpiece.

'Look at it this way; if you hadn't, then his girl friend wouldn't have heard you sing.'

'I expect she'll forget all about me.'

'I doubt it. You weren't exactly forgettable.'

Claudia started to laugh; then she turned round and Rod saw she was crying too. She went towards him and fell against his chest, her laughter extinguished by sobs.

'Hey, come on!'

'I hate myself, I hate myself, I hate myself. You're the best person in my life, and all I do is hurt you. Gerry is a swine, but he's only got to say run and I run—to him. I hate myself.'

'Why did you hit him?'

'Because—never mind. It's not important.'

'It looked as if it was.'

'I hit him because of the whole of last year; I hit him because he won't take me seriously; I hit him because sometimes I feel he's destroying me—'

Rod pushed her away. 'You make me angry. Nothing will destroy you. You're being self-indulgent and ridiculous. Why the hell should it matter if he doesn't take you seriously, if he doesn't come and hear you sing? Your pride is wounded, dear Claudia, that's what's biting you.'

She stared at him, tears still on her cheeks. There was a long silence. Then Rod, unable to help himself, yawned. He rubbed his face. 'I'm knackered. I'm suddenly so knackered I can hardly stand up.'

Claudia stared at him for a few seconds longer, and then with a twist of her mouth she ran out of the room and banged the front door behind her.

*List of recommendations in no particular order
for the daily consideration of Miss Claudia Dalton*

1. *Never get emotionally involved.*
2. *If you do (more fool you) learn to pretend successfully that you haven't.*
3. *Think before you hit out.*
4. *Leave home as soon as possible.*
5. *Learn some self-discipline.*
6. *Never forget the most important thing in your life is your voice.*
7. *Be kinder.*
8. *Eat less.*
9. *Cure yourself of your bad habits: picking gunge out of your ears, chewing your hair, saying despair despair the whole time.*
10. *Etc. Etc. Etc. . . . and don't take this list too seriously.*

14

Rod woke up very early on Sunday morning. He was cold and stiff. Unfamiliar patterns of light made him wonder where he was; then he saw the shutters and remembered. He tried to go back to sleep, but the camp bed remained obdurately uncomfortable; it collapsed as he got out of it. He went through into the old kitchen where he found the end of a packet of biscuits. He ate these standing at the back door.

The sun was still low, but the sky very clear. Doves cooed; a fox sauntered across the far end of the lawn. Rod felt his tiredness lift in the utterly peaceful surroundings. He sat for some time on the doorstep, going over in his mind the previous evening's happenings.

He must leave soon. Today. Tomorrow. No later than tomorrow. It was time he went south again. He had become obsessed with his life in Yorkshire, obsessed. It had been such a full month. He had even stopped thinking about his father: that pain was gone. He gazed out at the quiet garden; yes, that pain had truly gone. Sitting in the morning sun with his back against the door-jamb, he shut his eyes and time passed.

Henry's files. Something in the slow passage of his thoughts reminded him that he had left a pile of Henry's files under a yew tree. He ought to burn them; he hoped Henry had not found them. He got up, and took a large box of matches from the kitchen table. He would burn the files now, if the paper wasn't too damp. He picked up a copy of the *Daily Mirror* left behind by the removal men; that would help start the fire.

Quietly he made his way through the door in the garden wall into the churchyard. The yew tree was beyond a privet hedge;

as he drew nearer, he froze. Someone was behind the hedge, muttering.

'Ah, Richard, how I have failed thee.'

It was Henry's voice. Rod's hair prickled; he could not move. He heard paper rustling.

'Vanity, all vanity. I will never do it.' Clicks and more rustling. 'Dear God. The right thing for the wrong reason.'

Rod tried to creep away unseen. He had only taken three steps when Henry straightened up beyond the hedge. He was in his cassock; his black figure stood out against the soft morning light.

'Ah, Rod.' His face was gaunt, but he tried to smile. 'Lovely morning, isn't it?'

'Yes.'

'You're up early.'

'I don't even know what the time is.'

'Oh, seven thirty-ish. I've just celebrated the seven o'clock communion. Coming for some breakfast?' But he did not move. Rod went up to the hedge.

'I'm sorry about those files. We were interrupted and then we forgot to burn them. I put them under the yew tree.'

'Couldn't think at first what they were.' Several of the files were open at Henry's feet.

'I thought I'd burn them now.'

'Good idea.' He started to stack them in his arms. He looked dispirited.

'Perhaps you'd like to keep these few after all?'

'Burn them. I'll help you.'

After their little bonfire, they walked over to the new house and made themselves some breakfast. As Henry stirred the leaves in the teapot, he asked, 'What are your plans now, Rod? Do stay here as long as you like, of course.'

'Thanks, but I must get back to London. I thought I'd go tomorrow.'

'I'm driving into York on Tuesday. I could give you a lift there.' He sat down on a crate with his mug of tea.

'Thanks, that would be good.' An extra day; he viewed this with mixed feelings. If only Claudia were predictable.

Claudia did not appear until lunchtime; while the rest of the Daltons went to church, Rod returned to the old house, put the camp bed back together, and lay morosely reading a thriller with half his attention. His sense of anticlimax was so strong that part of him wanted to leave for London immediately. Perhaps he could invent a sudden urgent phone call from his family . . . he dozed off.

At lunch Claudia was equally morose. 'This house gets me down. It's so uncomfortable.'

'That's only because we haven't organized ourselves,' said Henry. 'When books are out and pictures are hung you'll see the difference.'

'It'll still be too small, nastily built and too full of furniture.'

'Oh, do stop complaining, Claudia.' Di was sharp.

The telephone rang. None of the Daltons moved, each waiting for another to answer it. Evelyn was the first to crack; she yelled from the hall that it was Angela someone for Claudia.

As Claudia ran out she caught Rod's eye briefly. She returned after five minutes pink with excitement.

'It's Gerry's friend, Angela Barker—she wants me to go to York and meet a teacher of singing—she suggested I went tomorrow—what do you think?'

'I can take you to York on Tuesday. Fix it for then. I've got to be there by eleven. Rod's coming too.'

Claudia went back to the phone, and wrote down the arrangements as they were made. She danced back into the kitchen.

'Well, what about that then. I am going to this Oriana Donskova woman at midday. If she likes my voice enough she might take me on. She has apparently taught lots of famous people in her time. Even though she's old and retired now, Angela says her voice is still amazing.' Claudia stopped and looked round the silent room. 'You are a stuffy lot. I get my big break and no one is interested.'

165

'We are, *of course* we are.' Di spoke; Henry gazed at Claudia over the Sunday paper. 'It would be good for you to be properly taught. I'm just a little worried she might be astronomically expensive.'

'The money doesn't matter, Ma. I can pay myself.'

Henry put down the paper. 'What with? She could easily cost a great deal more than you realize.'

'I've saved up a great deal more than you realize.' Claudia gazed defiantly back at her father. 'I have saved it so that one day I could pay someone good to teach me to sing.'

Henry was nonplussed. Josephine said immediately: 'How much?'

'Nearly three hundred pounds.'

There was a complete silence, broken finally by Di. 'How?'

'I've been saving for years.'

'But so much . . .'

Claudia shrugged. 'Well, I haven't pinched any of it.'

Henry said at last: 'You amaze me. How long have you been determined to learn to sing?'

Rod watched Claudia's face. He thought she was going to refuse an answer; she looked sideways at her father as if assessing him. He stared back.

'Since I was fourteen.'

'What gave you the idea?'

'You don't believe in my voice, do you?'

'Claudia, give me time. I only asked what made you start saving money for a teacher.'

'It doesn't matter. Once I knew, I didn't waver. But I had to keep it secret, otherwise I knew you'd have all undermined me. Now there's no point keeping it a secret any more, not after last night.'

'What happened last night?' Josephine looked uneasily at Claudia.

'Your sister was a wild success. She surprised us all.'

'Not me,' said Rod.

All the Daltons except Claudia turned towards him; in their

166

interest at her revelations, they had forgotten he was there. Despite his embarrassment, he went on: 'I knew the moment I first heard her she was out of the ordinary.'

Henry stood up; he had obviously had enough. 'Well, we all know how difficult it is to be a prophet in one's own country. Good for you, Claudia. Now, to work. All hands to the plough.' He went up to the study and began to unpack books.

Di put an arm round Rod. 'Thank you for your perspicacity. I suspect that a good part of last night's success was due to you.'

From the sink, Claudia said over her shoulder: 'Dead right.'

'What did give you the idea?'

'Is *snorkelize* a word?'

'No.'

'I wanted to use up my Z.'

'Go on, tell me, Claudia, what did give you the idea?'

'What idea?'

'Never mind. I don't really want to know.'

Claudia laughed at Rod. 'You wouldn't be asking me about it if you didn't. *Zone*. There. I've only got one letter left.'

'*Ozone*. Double word score too.'

'Clever old you. There, I'm out. You add up the totals.'

She watched him do this with what seemed to her fantastic speed. 'Who's won?'

'I have, by a small margin. *Ozone* did the trick.'

'I never win at Scrabble.' Claudia stretched herself. 'All right, I'll tell you how it all began. Not that it's a very exciting story anyway. It was all because of a French teacher at school called Mrs Fellows. She used to play us French songs at the end of each term. Jacques Brel, Charles Trenet, Edith Piaf—but mainly Piaf. That's why I'm mad on Piaf. At first when I heard any French songs I wasn't very impressed: they seemed difficult, unapproachable somehow. But after a while I began to see what Mrs Fellows was on about. She always said she liked singers who sang with heart *and* brain, and that most pop singers were short of both, though full of sentimentality. And she also made us see how good the words were, by giving us songs to translate. I remember doing *The Three Bells*, and *Padam, Padam*.'

'I know *The Three Bells*. I love it.'

'*Padam, Padam*'s good too.' Claudia hummed the catchy tune. 'I taught myself to sing it. It's a song about Piaf's past, her memories. Her voice is amazing; I realized how special when I tried to copy it.'

'Sing *Padam* now.'

'I couldn't. I've honestly forgotten the words. Anyway. Through doing all this I got hooked on the idea that a woman could show such passion and pain and—oh, I don't know—gutsiness through her voice, beyond just the beauty of sound. And since I realized I had the basic ingredient, a good voice, I promised myself I'd do the same. Whenever I hear the voices of singers like Maria Callas or Ella Fitzgerald or Piaf, it's the fact that they sing with the *whole* of themselves that really excites me.' Claudia jumped up and paced about. 'Most people are so half-hearted by comparison. I know I am.'

'No one could call you half-hearted, Claudia. Many other things, but not that.'

'Well, *you* could. I've been half-hearted to you.'

'That wasn't quite what I was talking about.' Rod doodled busily on the sheet of paper bearing their scores. 'But since we're on that subject—do you think you might feel more whole-hearted towards me when you've got over Gerry?' He did not look at her.

'I don't know, Rod. I won't know until I have got over him, and at the moment I feel I never will. I cringe when I think of slapping him yesterday—'

'Don't go on about that.'

'I'm sorry. Oh, Rod, of all the people I've ever met you're the one I feel most relaxed with.'

'Thanks.'

'It's a compliment.'

'It doesn't really feel like one.'

'Well, it is.'

'Kiss me.'

'No.' She sat down again.

'You'll never change towards me. To you, I'm just a soft, undemanding cushion you can relax against.'

'Quite wrong. And I will change. To use a corny old expression, there's only room for one love in my heart at a time.'

The clock struck midnight; when it had finished, Rod said: 'So what's going to happen in York on Tuesday? Tell me the arrangements.'

'Angela Barker is taking me to Oriana Donskova's house, to introduce me. Then I wow her with my singing and she says,'— Claudia struck an attitude—'You hef ze most vonderful voice I hef effer heard. You must gif up everysing to study singing. You vill be a star.' Claudia giggled. 'She's more likely to tell me politely to push off and not waste her time.'

'You don't believe that.'

'No, I suppose I don't, but it could happen.'

'If she takes you on—'

'Don't let's speculate.'

'I'm going for a walk.' Rod unwound suddenly from his chair.

'It's very late.'

'I feel wide awake.'

Claudia lay in her chair, humming *Padam, Padam*. 'I'll come too.' But she did not move. Rod went to the door.

'I'd rather go on my own.'

'Fine.' They stared for a moment at each other. 'Please believe me, Rod. You mean a lot to me.'

Padam, Padam. He went out into the windy night.

I wish I hadn't worn this dress. I don't feel happy in it. It's too long for a start, and I'm beginning to think yellow isn't my colour. And I've torn my nail and it's all jagged. And to cap it all I've got the curse. Life's against me, it really is.

Oh God, I feel quite sick at the thought of this audition. What if she says I'm no good? Or if she says I've got a pretty voice but it's not good enough to take further? Do I accept her judgement and give up the idea of being a professional singer; do I take no notice and go on regardless? She's just an old woman who's retired and might not be in touch any more . . . Oriana Donskova. She sounds Russian.

'I'm going to use the car park down near the castle. Where are you meeting Gerry's friend?'

'Outside the West door of the Minster at quarter to twelve.'

'You'll have time to show Rod something of York then. I should concentrate on the Minster.'

'Yes, Dad.'

'That is, if Rod hasn't seen it?'

'No, *never*.'

Gerry's friend. I wonder why she's being so particularly kind to me. Perhaps she feels sorry for me. Ugh. What a thought. Oh well. Rod's right, though, I mustn't be rude to her. It's stupid to show my jealously like that. Charm her, Claudia. Charm her. She'll wonder what's behind it.

'. . . there's been a church of some sort on the site since 627. The Minster itself is Medieval Gothic—it's the largest medieval cathedral in Britain . . .'

'Really . . .'

'And it also has one of the largest stained glass windows in the world . . .'

Seventy-six feet high and thirty-two feet wide. Oh, Dad, we could all give your talk on the dear old Minster, we've heard it so often. Hell, the way I'm feeling at this minute, I'd rather go on a guided tour round the Minster than sing to an operatic Russian.

15

When they left the car park, Rod offered Claudia a coffee. He took her into a sandwich bar in High Ousegate, enjoying the sensation of following her through the door; he liked her yellow dress, and the way she had done her hair, soft and loose with two small sections plaited each side and drawn over her hair to the back of her head. She was very pale this morning; he liked that too.

'Never get suntanned.'

She looked up in surprise at his abrupt remark made as they settled themselves next to each other at a table.

'Whatever made you say that?'

'I like your skin white. I can never understand the craze for going brown. My sister Julia lies in the garden for hours, basting herself with oil.'

'I never go brown anyway.'

'Good.' He felt happy sitting beside her, drinking rather good coffee. She drained her cup very quickly, and he offered her another.

'I'd love one. I needed this. I should have had more breakfast.'

So he fetched a second cup and folded himself onto the bench closer to her.

'What are you going to sing for this lady?'

'*Plaisir d'Amour.*'

'Good idea.'

'If she wants any more, perhaps you'd accompany me?'

'You're not expecting me to come too, are you? I mean, I'm sure she won't want me there as well.'

'Why not? Please, Rod. I'm sure she won't mind. Then I can come and see you off afterwards. What time did you say your train went?'

'Just after two.' A train to London. The prospect wasn't credible. 'But I can get a later one if I miss it.'

'Aren't you being met?'

'I told Mum not to bother. I suppose she might come anyway.'

'Then you mustn't miss your train.'

They murmured peacefully to each other, and time slipped by until Rod realized it was a quarter to twelve, when they were supposed to meet Angela Barker. They tore through the streets to the Minster, and found her looking rather annoyed outside the great West door.

'I thought you'd got lost.'

'Sorry we're late.'

'I didn't expect you to be here as well,' she said to Rod. He felt foolish, and wished he had not let Claudia persuade him to come. He should have caught an earlier train. He heard Claudia say:

'Do you think she'll mind if Rod sits in?'

Angela hesitated. 'She's a strange person. She can be very brusque if she's annoyed. I should play it by ear.' She talked on, telling them where she'd first met Oriana Donskova; she was witty and articulate, and put neither of them at their ease. Claudia met Rod's eye when they were crossing a road in her wake. He hoped Angela was not also hoping to sit in on the audition.

They had passed through the city wall at Monk Bar, and turned into a street off to the left when Angela said: 'There she is.'

A sandy-haired old woman was leaning out of a first-floor window shaking a Paisley shawl. Angela waved.

'Oriana! We've arrived!'

'The cat has covered this with hairs.' The old woman shook the shawl again, and then withdrew. They waited for several minutes before the front door opened, and Oriana Donskova came out to greet them.

'This is Claudia Dalton, Oriana, the singer I so wanted you to meet.'

'You're younger than I expected.' She had lively clear blue eyes sunk in a lined and haggard face. She stared for a moment and then switched her gaze to Rod. 'Another singer?'

'This is my accompanist, Rod Parrish.' Claudia's yellow dress billowed out in the wind. 'Could he possibly come in while I have my audition?'

Rod felt like walking off down the street; he opened his mouth to say it didn't matter, but the old lady suddenly beamed at him. 'Of course he can come in. I don't see enough young men. He's welcome.' She stepped back towards the door. 'Now, Angela, I know you said you couldn't linger, so we won't keep you. Thank you so much for bringing these young people—'

'Oh, well, no trouble—' Angela, put out, managed to wave before the door was firmly closed leaving her outside.

'Claudia. Rod. Follow me.' With surprising speed Oriana Donskova led them upstairs and into a large, long room with windows at both ends. At one end of the room was a delicate gold-painted fourposter bed; on its green velvet cover lay the Paisley shawl. At the other end of the room was a grand piano, also draped with a shawl, this time of black silk with red flowers. The walls of the room were covered with framed photographs, posters and programmes; there was even a ticket-stub in a tiny square frame. Rod noticed written below the stub: 'Emmy Destinn's last performance at Covent Garden in *Aida*, 1919'.

There were fronds everywhere—potted ferns, a great jar full of dried palm leaves, plumed feathers tucked behind some of the pictures. On the floor near an ornate sideboard were piles of scores and libretti.

'What confusion!' Oriana Donskova stepped over the piles. 'I've just been sorting through these, looking for a Rossini

174

libretto. In vain.'

Claudia and Rod stood in silence, awed by her room and the evidence it held of a richly distinctive life.

'Now. First I'll hear you sing.' Her gingery-grey hair stood up like a halo against the light of the window behind her. 'Angela tells me you gave a concert the other night. What did you sing?'

Claudia told her, and Oriana Donskova listened with a non-committal expression.

'Oh, I see. Popular folk songs. Well, never mind, sing. It's your voice I want to hear. Do you want me to play the piano for you?'

Claudia shook her head. 'I'll sing *Plaisir d'Amour* unaccompanied.'

'Begin when you are quite, quite ready. I will sit on the bed with your friend.'

Rod guessed Claudia was nervous, but it was hard to be sure. She stood very straight, breathing evenly. As had happened at the cabaret, her stillness caught the attention. But when she started to sing, her first few notes were rough; she grew steadier but was not in her best voice. Rod felt tension spreading through him; he could not bear the possibility that this rather fearsome old lady should misjudge Claudia on today's evidence.

When she had finished, there was a short silence. Then Oriana Donskova stood up and said briskly without commenting on Claudia's performance, 'Now. Let us establish your range.' She went over to the piano and played an arpeggio, starting on a note so low that Claudia sang it with difficulty. They progressed up the piano with a series of arpeggios.

'Don't snatch at the notes. Relax. Open your throat. Open it. Feel the space in your head.'

Claudia was now singing better; she sang high notes Rod had never heard her reach before.

'That will do.' Oriana swivelled on her piano stool. 'Don't force those high notes. They will come. There's no point

175

screeching them, is there?' She sat for a moment, her hands on her knees. Claudia asked her nervously:

'Am I a soprano, or a mezzo? It's silly, but I don't really know—'

'It's not silly. Your voice is still unformed. Even putting it into a category isn't very helpful, but I would say you are a high mezzo at the moment, with all the chances that you will find you end up a soprano—a dramatic not a lyric soprano. I can at least say with certainty you will never be a *soprano lirico*.'

'They never let me sing soprano at school—'

'Ah, school. You are lucky they did not discover you and exploit you. Fourteen-year-olds singing Gilbert and Sullivan. Ruination. Now tell me, who has been your singing teacher?'

'No one.'

'Ah. That will explain the fact that your breath-control is non-existent. When you get a phrase right, I think it is by happy accident.'

Claudia grinned. Rod could now see she was nervous; she kept pulling a lock of hair forward and chewing it.

Oriana rootled through some sheet music on the piano. 'Can you sight-read?'

'A little.'

'Sing this. Don't worry if you make a mess of it, just try it. It's an aria by Puccini, *O mio babbino caro*—you might find it familiar. I'll transpose it so that it's within your range.'

Claudia mangled the Italian, but coped adequately with the notes; both she and Rod found the tune familiar, even though they had not known before what it was.

'Not bad, my child. What instrument do you play?'

'I began learning piano, but my younger sister was so much better than me I gave up.'

'Go back and learn it again. You must be able to play the piano, even badly. I maintain it is essential for a singer.' Oriana shut the piano. 'I have to keep the lid down because my cat is very fond of sitting on the keys.' There was a pause, broken by Claudia.

176

'Will I do?'

'Will you do what?'

'I mean, am I good enough? Would you take me as your pupil?'

Oriana laughed, showing several gold-capped teeth as she did so. 'I would have sent you out after your first song if I had not thought you had potential. You are *not* good enough, but you do have potential. You are undisciplined; you have some bad habits; you are too easily satisfied. I am probably mad even to consider taking you on—'

'But you will, please say you will—'

Oriana got up off the stool, and went to kiss her cheek. 'Don't look so desperate. Of course I will. Real potential is a challenge I can't resist. Now, let us all have a little something to celebrate, and then perhaps your friend would like to amuse himself while I give you a preliminary lesson and arrange our immediate future?'

'Yes, I'll go and look at the Minster.'

'You are not a local?' Oriana fetched glasses and a half-empty bottle of wine from a cupboard.

'No, I'm a Londoner. I'm going back this afternoon.'

'Not hitchhiking, I hope—'

'No, by train.'

'Never hitchhike. I have a horror of it. Only the other day I heard a terrible story—a young man was given a lift by two middle-aged women, nice quiet-looking women, and do you know what they did? They took him to a nice quiet spot, and castrated him, that's what they did.' Oriana poured wine out. 'This is a bit flat but never mind.' She handed them their glasses. 'So never hitchhike. Now, let's drink to Claudia's *potential* voice. But never forget, I say this to all aspiring singers, never forget that however beautiful your natural voice, to develop it to its full and true expression is a long, hard road.'

Claudia raised her glass. 'To a long, hard road. And I don't care how hard.'

'*Long* is the important adjective, my dear. Long. These days

177

everyone starts their public singing career much too soon, and if they are any good they are flooded with offers—Vienna, Milan, New York, London—and they are finished by the time they reach thirty-five.'

'Thirty-five . . .'

Oriana prodded Claudia. 'I can read your thoughts. You may think thirty-five is too old anyway, but let me tell you, many singers are in their prime then, and continue to sing magnificently for ten and more years. Melba was singing beautifully, but beautifully, in her fifties.' She paused, then swept across the room and pointed to the framed ticket stub. 'Emmy Destinn. There's a story to show the dangers of starting your career too young.'

'Who was Emmy Destinn?' Rod felt it was expected he should ask the question; Claudia sat enraptured by everything Oriana said. He on the other hand was beginning to feel impatient at Oriana's rather florid manner.

'A great soprano, dear boy, who sang all over Europe before the First World War.'

'That notice says 1919—'

'Indeed it does. She came back to Covent Garden to sing *Aida*. I was taken to hear her: I was seventeen. I shall never forget her though she was past her best then. Only forty, but her career was nearly over. She began to sing in public very early, when she was only nineteen. She sang big demanding roles too early, too early.'

Rod sipped his rather acid wine and listened to Oriana telling Claudia at length about early operatic prima donnas. He felt excluded. His glance wandered along the walls, seeing photographs of stocky tenors dressed in tights and doublet, of bosomy women curiously corseted, of Oriana herself in Japanese dress in *Madam Butterfly*. The atmosphere in the room was overpowering.

'I ought to go now.' He broke into Oriana's monologue. 'I'd like to see a bit of York before my train.'

'Of course, of course. Off you go.'

178

'I'll meet you down at the station, Rod. Ten to two?'

'Fine. I'll let myself out, don't worry.'

'Goodbye, dear boy. Nice to have met you.' Oriana had a big scrapbook on her knee, with a finger jammed in to mark her place.

'Well, goodbye. Thanks for the wine.'

As Rod went out Oriana began again; opening up the scrapbook: 'Of course Rosa Ponselle didn't have the acting ability of say, Callas—' Their two heads bent over the scrapbook. While Rod went downstairs, Oriana's voice continued to describe the nature of this Rosa Ponselle. A cat shot past him, nearly tripping him up. When he picked up his rucksack and opened the front door, it rushed into the street. He did not care whether this exodus was permitted or not. Let the old witch's cat get lost. He then saw it go into the basement area and climb straight back into the house through an open window.

At a corner shop he bought a meat pie and an apple, and walked back up Monkgate. He ate his lunch in the Minster park, sitting on a bench under huge plane trees and staring up at the bulk of the cathedral. Henry's description in the car had fired his interest, and when he had eaten he hurried round to the great West front. People were passing through the big wooden doors. Surprised by such a crowd, he followed. A verger asked for his ticket, and explained a special service was about to start. 'No admission except by ticket.'

'But—'

The verger was politely adamant. 'You can go through the East door, sir, and climb the tower or look at the undercroft. But the main cathedral is closed for the moment.'

Excluded again, and desolate, Rod wandered round the building. He discovered that climbing the tower cost 50p, and visiting the undercroft 40p. He hesitated, counting his change. He had less than he expected. He went out again into the street.

'Ah, that telephone. Excuse me, Claudia.'

She's more amazing than I ever dreamed. I suppose she's Russian, though she doesn't have any accent. And her voice, at seventy-whatever-she-is—I can't get over it. She looked so good on the stage when she was young. Really quite beautiful in that photograph. And what was the name of the singer who looks like me—which page was it?—there she is—Conchita Supervia. Died in childbirth at 40. What a waste. She looks fabulous as Carmen . . .

'Sorry about that, Claudia. What were we talking about?'

'When did this Conchita Supervia sing?'

'Oh, in the thirties. Now close that scrapbook. Forget all the stars of the past and let's concentrate on the present. To work. I am an eccentric and autocratic old lady, I warn you. Either you work my way, or we part good friends now.'

'I'll work your way.'

'Lie down on the floor. I want to see you breathe, to see your diaphragm muscles working. Now, breathe in. Hold. Let your breath out in controlled little puffs. Again. Again. Relax, Dear girl, you take breaths as if you are blowing up a balloon. Too rough, too stiff. Look—your shoulders. Like a tin soldier. Relax.'

'I am relaxed.'

'No, you are tense. You think you are relaxed but I assure you, you are not. Now, let's begin again . . .'

This is somehow not a bit what I expected of a first singing lesson . . . I am discovering muscles in my head and neck and chest I never knew I had.

180

'*That is enough for the first time. Now we must discuss arrangements. What are those exams you say you must take again?*'

'*Just my A-levels. I need them to get into university. Or perhaps I ought to try for a college of music—*'

'*University. Start there. Most singers are abominably educated. You can always specialize later. That's my advice.*'

'*And of course I can do a lot of singing if I get into the right university for it—*'

'*Singing?*'

'*In choirs and things.*'

'*No choirs. Absolutely no choirs. They can ruin your voice.*'

'*But—*'

'*Certainly go to university, study any subject, History, languages—indeed, languages would be good. Italian, German, French . . . But please don't join any amateur choirs. I know it's fun singing in oratorios, but you can so easily hurt your vocal chords. No one corrects you if your technique is wrong. Ah no, not that telephone again. One day I will tear it out of the wall. Excuse me.*'

Miss Oriana Donskova as Mimi, Metropolitan Opera House, New York, 1927. Ditto as Gilda, 'Rigoletto', Paris Opéra . . . *oh, oh, oh. It blows my mind. I had no idea she was such a star herself . . .*

'*Shut that scrapbook, bad girl. I told you to leave it alone. I will show it all to you one day but not now.*'

'*Were you born in Russia? You are Russian, aren't you—*'

'*I'm no more Russian than you are. I was born in Scarborough, with the name of Ethel Botcher. When I was twenty I decided I needed a more romantic name if I were going to make a career as a singer. Of course, these days people don't worry; they use the name they've got, however plain it is. You're lucky anyway—Claudia Dalton is a good, memorable name. Claudia Dalton. Yes. I wouldn't have changed my name if it had been yours. But now you must shut that scrapbook and I must stop reminiscing. We have arrangements to discuss.*'

181

'Oh, all these photographs show such an exciting world, the most exciting—'

'Don't exaggerate it. You are like me, you exaggerate everything. But then, that is what I like: it's better to teach discipline to a big passionate temperament than to draw passion out of a disciplined mouse. You can laugh—I have had pupils with souls the size of dried peas. But, down to details. How are you going to get to York for lessons, keep your studies going, and manage to work, work, work, at this voice you have?'

'I don't know yet, but I'll find a solution. I'll have to talk to my parents—'

'I have an idea. I'm not sure if it's a good idea, either for you or for me, but it could be. It could be. I used to have a lodger upstairs. Max lives downstairs, but the upstairs room is empty because I have had some bad experiences with students. If you can find a tutorial college for your schoolwork, you could live here, and then our singing lessons would be no problem. But there is another problem: you are young, and I am sure you haven't lived away from home before. I am not a motherly person, dear Claudia. If you are not self-sufficient and independent, you could be very unhappy here. You haven't left home before, have you?'

'No, but it's time I did. I'm sure my parents will heave a sigh of relief if I leave home. Anyway, I'm fed up with family life.'

'All young people are fed up with family life. That's not the point. They may be fed up, but they are not always ready to leave it. If you live here, you will be on your own. I cannot be responsible for you, only for your singing lessons. I'm too old and too selfish to start being a surrogate mother. You will have to cater and clean for yourself.'

'I'd cope. If you like, I could bring my father to see you. He's in York today on business. Then we could all discuss your suggestion together.'

'Only, Claudia, if you are sure in your own mind.'

'I'm positive. I'd adore living here.'

'Then yes, bring him.'

'Did Angela tell you my father is a priest?'

'She didn't, but what difference does that make?'

'None, except we don't have much money. I've saved up nearly three hundred pounds to pay for my lessons, but I don't think that would pay for my board as well for very long. We never seem to have enough at home for extras. I—I'm sorry to tell you all this, but money stops our family from doing lots of things we want to.'

'Ah, money. How I hate it. All my life it's been money, money; you can't do this, not enough money; pay me more money; accept less money; on and on. But my needs are few now, thank God; I don't need much money any more. Claudia, perhaps you are my swansong. Why should money stop us? You have done very well to save so much at your age; we'll make it last. I will give you a room and lessons for a fee that will suit us both; your parents will pay for everything else just as they would if you were living at home. We'll manage. I think we'll manage beautifully. No, no, don't be ridiculous. It's my pleasure. I have a feeling I won't regret it. If I do, I'll throw you out . . .'

16

Rod crossed over the Ouse and wandered along North Street. He still had time to kill before his train left. He saw a tall steeple ahead of him: another ancient church. Never had he been in a place with so many old churches. Bewildered by their number he had hesitated outside those he had passed and then entered none of them. He read the sign ahead of him: All Saints' Church. Its worn, beautifully structured stone had settled delicately on the earth; the steeple continued the illusion of delicacy. Without further thought, Rod entered the churchyard and found the main door.

The interior took him by surprise. Colour dazzled him; it streamed through the many stained glass windows, it sang from the roof above him. The hammer beams and bosses were freshly restored to their original medieval colours: scarlet, leaf green, cobalt, pale blue glowed against white, black and gold leaf. Vivid faces leered down at him; one, his red lips stretched wide by his hands, stuck out an even redder fat tongue. Brightly painted angels with large gold wings played instruments; animals listened. Rod stood entranced, his desolation temporarily forgotten.

The stained glass windows were equally eye-catching; people with lively medieval faces and richly coloured clothes acted out their permanent story. Rod saw with delight a man wearing spectacles in a window of fifteenth-century glass. He drifted on round the church until he came to a notice informing him that above was the *Pricke of Conscience* window, illustrating the last fifteen days of the world as described by the great mystic Richard Rolle in his poem of the same name . . .

Rod gave an involuntary exclamation, as if he had met a friend in an unexpected place. The window was strange, full of mysterious scenes, of clumsy falling stars and thick tongues of flame, of trees and rocks drawn as if by a child. Rod could sort no sequence out. He gazed at the grandiose yet homely vision of chaos, and felt suddenly close to the medieval world in which Rolle had lived. The whole of this small church seemed to sum up its combination of earthbound practical piety and spiritual power.

Rod sat down on a stone ledge, and leant back closing his eyes. Oh Yorkshire, Yorkshire. Abbeys and churches, mystics and moors; yet superimposed on his mind full of images was Claudia. He yearned for her; as he sat in the musty corner beneath the beams of coloured light, he ached for her. He was mad to feel so strongly about her; he knew there would always be something to distance her from him. It wasn't so much Gerry he was afraid of, but her growing absorption with singing, with her voice. The implications of this brought back his sense of desolation; he sat with body and mind fused in misery.

Footsteps disturbed him; a group of people had arrived to look at the church. Rod left quickly, realizing as he did so that he was now short of time; he ran in the direction of the station, but the route was roundabout and took him longer than he expected. When he saw the time on the station clock he hoped Claudia would be waiting for him. He rushed up and down looking for her, but there was no sign of her. Ten minutes to his train. He stood at the entrance of the station staring up towards the Minster. People pushed past him; a coachload disembarked all round him. He had to move back into the entrance hall out of their way. He was aware of the passage of each minute, each second; if she came now he would hardly see her. A man tripped against his guitar and he bent to retrieve it.

'*Rod!* Rod. I'm sorry—'

'We've got five minutes.'

'How lovely—I thought I was going to miss you altogether.

185

Let's go straight onto the platform.'

'Did you forget?'

'Of course not. O.D. booted me out anyway because she'd had enough. I didn't leave enough time to get here, that's all. I thought it would only take five minutes. Oh Rod, quick, let me tell you the best—not only is she going to teach me but I'm going to lodge in her house for next year, and take my A-levels through a tutorial college in York. Escape from home at last! Singing lessons twice a week as well as living in York which is one of my favourite places—'

'Lucky you.'

They pushed their way onto the crowded platform. People were already craning to see if the train was coming. Claudia took Rod's arm.

'I was so afraid I'd miss you altogether.'

'You nearly did.'

'Oh Rod. Cheer up. I can't help feeling high today—feel high with me. Let's get together at Christmas. I'll come and stay with you in London as you suggested. I'd love that.'

'Promise you'll come.'

'Of course I will. Rod, Oriana is *fantastic*. She knows so much about singing—it's the luckiest thing for me that I've met her. She's—'

'Here's the train.'

'Damn it for being on time. Despair, despair.'

Claudia turned to hug him; they clung together until the rush of people round them jostled them apart.

'Quick, get in or you'll never get a seat. It's very full.'

'I don't mind. I'll sit in the corridor.'

He kissed her; they gazed at each other.

'I'll miss you.'

'I'll miss you too.'

'No, you won't. You'll be too busy singing your head off.'

'I *will* miss you.'

'Till Christmas.'

'Yes.'

Rod jumped on the train as it began to pull out. Claudia ran beside it, her face full of excitement and warmth. They managed to touch hands briefly; then she laughed and slowed down. He leant out for as long as he could see her, and then stood gazing sightlessly through the window as the suburbs of York slipped past.